I AM SPECIAL TOO!

A Circle of Angels
WORKBOOK

*designed for the little people of the world,
waiting to join and share in the light*

Written & Illustrated by
Leia A. Stinnett

Other Books by Leia Stinnett:

The Twelve Universal Laws

The Little Angel Books Series:
The Angel Told Me to Tell You Good-bye
The Bridges Between Two Worlds
Color Me One
Crystals R for Kids   8/0 3
Exploring the Chakras
Happy Feet
One Red Rose
When the Earth Was New
Where Is God?
Who's Afraid of the Dark?

All My Angel Friends (Coloring Book)

Cover art
by Leia Stinnett

ISBN 0-929385-87-X

Published by

StarChild Press
a division of
Light Technology Publishing
P.O. Box 1526
Sedona, Arizona 86339
(520) 282-6523

Printed by
MISSION POSSIBLE
Commercial
Printing
P.O. Box 1495
Sedona, AZ 86339

DEDICATION

This workbook is dedicated to all
the little people of the world who
with their innocence carry the
great task of working toward the
enlightenment of all mankind . . .

. . . To my loving daughter Christina,
in whose eyes I saw the importance
of accomplishing this task
for the children of the world . . .

. . . And to my loving companion
Douglas Stinnett, without whose love,
light, encouragement and support this
workbook would not be possible.

May God share with each and every
one of you His/Her eternal light
of peace, love and
never-ending happiness.

A NOTE TO PARENTS . . .

Planet Earth is now entering the Aquarian Age of peace, joy and harmony among all men and women . . . but it is not an easy transition from the Piscean Age of division. As institutions, religions and structures of Earth divide in the next one hundred years as predicted, it will be the task of the lightworkers to assist mankind in its reach for spiritual awareness. And the lightworkers I speak of at this writing are the children of Earth today — yours and mine.

Our children are very old souls. They are very aware. Whether you as parents realize it or not, they know a great deal more about God, the universe and enlightenment than you or I could ever imagine. Our role as parents at this time on the planet is to offer our children spiritual guidance . . . not following the rules, policies and regulations of our society, but allowing them to explore and expand their ways of thinking, according to divine law and guidance.

A Circle of Angels workbook is presented to the little people of the world waiting to join and share in the light. All children carry the light of God in their heart. If this workbook helps that light to expand and grow brighter in each child who reads and practices its contents, then this work shall have accomplished its task.

Let each child be a child of the universe, at one with all things . . . plants, animals, people . . . at one with God, the Source of All That Is. The greatest gift of our Creator is the love, peace and joy that a child brings to planet Earth. Let the light of each child shine on . . .

TABLE OF CONTENTS

ILLUSTRATIONS

MEDITATIONS

INTRODUCTION

In this workbook you will learn about energy . . . but not the same type of energy you are used to seeing in the form of sunlight, steam, electricity and so on. You will be learning about nonphysical energy called *psychic energy*.

How many times have you known who was calling on the telephone before you picked up the receiver? How many times did you know what your parents or a friend was going to say and you "took the words right out of their mouth"?

Do you see little balls of colored lights? Spirit friends? Angels? This is a natural part of yourself that you will learn more about in this workbook.

We are used to sensing things in the world around us with our physical senses — our eyes, ears, nose, hands and mouth. We can sense nonphysical things around us, but we use a different sensing system — our chakras — our body's energy centers. You will learn how to use your nonphysical sensing systems so you can practice to make them work better and better. Practice makes perfect, you know!

To better use this nonphysical sensing system, you will need to learn how to breathe properly, relax your body and mind, concentrate on only one thing at a time, and get into a state of mind we call an *altered state* — like daydreaming. You will learn these steps through meditation.

As you develop your ability to meditate, you will learn about the Source, or God, as you may prefer to call Him/Her, and how to connect with the Source for guidance. You will learn how to release uncomfortable feelings, do healing work on yourself and others, and connect with your spirit guides, guardian angels and spirit teachers — those special beings who are here to help you live life on Earth simply and happily.

You will learn how to sense energy in objects, including photographs, clothing and jewelry. You will learn how to see with your mind's eye, hear sounds in the spirit world, and send messages to another person with your mind.

Through working with crystals and stones, you will learn how to have better experiences in meditation, how to heal yourself and others, how to remember your dreams better, and how to keep your own energy systems balanced for maximum well-being.

So let's get started exploring that part of ourselves beyond our physical body.

1 • LEARNING TO MEDITATE

WHAT IS MEDITATION?

Meditation is a form of relaxation for the mind and body. When we meditate, we deepen our thoughts and feelings, and are thereby able to energize and heal our bodies. Meditation helps us change thoughts and feelings that make us feel bad to thoughts and feelings that make us feel good. Meditation takes us back to the Source of all life. It helps us become one with God.

There are three very simple ways to position the body to meditate.

First, you can use what is called the *lotus position*. Sit on the floor and cross your legs one over the other. When you sit like this, keep your back and spine very straight. Place your hands on your thighs or knees, palms up. This allows your body's energy to flow freely and evenly, helping you achieve more benefit from the meditation.

Second, you can sit in a chair with your feet flat on the floor. Keep your spine very straight. Place your hands on your thighs or knees, palms up.

Third, you can lie flat on your bed or the floor. Keep your back and spine straight and your legs uncrossed. Place your arms straight down at your side, palms up.

FIVE STEPS TO MEDITATION

1. Get into a relaxed position, keeping your spine very straight, either sitting up or lying down in a quiet place.
2. Close your eyes.
3. Begin to **breathe** very deeply and listen to your breathing or your heartbeat as you breathe in and out. Breathing helps you clear your mind of all thoughts.
4. **Relax** your entire body. Imagine relaxing energy at your toes and then see it move slowly up through your legs and hips right on up to the top of your head until you feel relaxed and calm all over.
5. **Focus** your mind on only one thought, feeling or idea. If any other thoughts come into your mind, simply let them flow right on out.

After this step you will find yourself in what is called an altered state of consciousness, like a place where you go when you daydream.

ENTERING AN ALTERED STATE MEDITATION

Get into a relaxed position, sitting or lying down. Close your eyes and listen very carefully to your breathing . . . in and out. Listen to your breathing as it slows down.

Now bring your attention to your heart. Listen to your heart beating inside your chest.

Breathe in very slowly through your nose, keeping your mouth closed. Count from 1 to 5 as you breathe in. Now hold your breath and again slowly count to 5. Then breathe out through your nose very slowly as you hold for 5 counts. In other words, breathe in to the count of 5, hold your breath to the count of 5 and then breathe out to the count of 5. Take 5 of these slow breaths.

Notice how your body is now beginning to feel calm and relaxed.

Be very still and quiet. With your mind, send some relaxing energy down to your toes. Then bring the relaxing energy up through your feet, your ankles and heels. Bring the relaxing energy up the calves of your legs, past your knees and into your thighs. Bring the relaxing energy up into your hips, the tip of your spine and around to your abdomen, stomach, chest and on up into your shoulders. Bring the relaxing energy down into your upper arms, past your elbows, into your forearms and down into your hands, through each finger and thumb to the very tips.

Now bring the relaxing energy up from your fingertips through your lower arms, past your elbows, into your upper arms and all the way back to the top of your shoulders. Then bring the energy up through your neck into your head and face.

Now your whole body is completely relaxed. Feel how relaxed you are.

Go deep within yourself to the center of your energy, your source, the center located about 3 inches above your bellybutton– the solar plexus. See the bright yellow color, as bright as the Sun. Feel the energy there. Feel the heat and see the beautiful light. Focus your attention on this center for a moment and keep your mind on the yellow light. Let all other thoughts simply pass through your mind.

Leave your center and move your attention up to your third eye, the center located between your eyebrows in the middle of your forehead. Stare right at the back of your eyes. See a beautiful, dark blue spot growing larger and larger. As you expand your awareness, the spot will also expand. Concentrate on making this spot as large and as blue as you can.

Now move your attention from your third eye center back to the center at your belly- button. Become aware of your heart beating in your chest, of your breathing, and of the room around you. Then open your eyes.

- Did you feel your body relax completely?
- Were you able to focus on the bright-yellow spot at your center?
- Did you see the blue spot in your third eye?
- Did you see anything or anyone else? What or who did you see?
- Did you hear anything? If so, what did you hear?
- Did you feel anything? What did you feel?

HEALING AND BALANCING USING COLORS

What is your favorite color?

Why do you like that particular color?

Do you like to wear or be around certain colors on certain days?

Did you ever think about why you like to wear or be around a certain color on a particular day, or why you have a favorite color?

Did you know that each color has a very special and unique kind of energy? Let's have fun with an experiment that will help you understand colors better.

EXERCISE IN FEELING COLORS

Ask your mom or dad to purchase some colored construction paper for you to practice with when you sense the energy of different colors. Choose a package that includes the colors red, orange, yellow, green, blue, indigo (dark blue), violet and white. Lay one sheet of each color on the floor. Close your eyes. Don't peek! Pick up one of the sheets, keeping your eyes closed. Hold the sheet of paper in your hand and concentrate very hard on what you are feeling.

How do you feel in your body? Do you feel warm? Cool? Calm? Energized? Happy? Sad? How do you feel?

With your eyes closed, can you see a color or picture? What do you see?

What color do you see or what color do you feel you are holding in your hand? After you know the color, open your eyes. Were you right? If not, try again. Keep practicing until you can choose the right color just by holding it in your hand, keeping your eyes closed.

Each different color, as we mentioned above, has a different energy around it. Each color feels different to us. When we look at the color or hold the color, we have a different feeling in our body.

When you look at the color red, how does it make you feel? Do you feel a lot of energy? Do you feel hot? Or do you feel angry?

When you look at the color blue, how does it make you feel? Do you feel more calm? Do you feel a bit "blue" or sad? Do you feel cool?

Each color of the rainbow vibrates at a different rate, or speed. Red is the lowest vibration and purple the highest vibration. Each color has some effect on the way we feel. We pick up the color's vibrations through our nonphysical sensors, through our body's abilities to sense or feel energy from people, places or objects.

MEDITATING WITH COLORS

The following meditation will help you change unwanted feelings that you have in your body or about yourself, to good feelings.

You can hold a crystal in your hands as you meditate, or just place your hands on your knees or thighs, palms up. The crystal will simply make your meditation stronger. It helps you imagine and see things more clearly as you meditate.

MEDITATION ON COLORS

To begin, look at the color chart on the next page and choose one of the colors that relates to the unwanted feelings you are experiencing in your body. When you have selected the color, sit on the floor in a lotus position (one leg crossed over the other) with your spine straight and your hands holding a crystal or resting on your knees or thighs, palms up.

Begin to breathe very deeply. Imagine your whole body becoming more and more relaxed and quiet. Start with your toes. Bring the relaxing energy right on up through each of your body parts to the top of your head.

Concentrate your mind on the color you have chosen from the chart. See the color. Feel the color. Be the color.

Now imagine yourself sitting in a pyramid. Your head is right under the point of the pyramid. Imagine the crystal, if you are holding one, filled with the color of your choice. Then, as you breathe, see the pyramid in which you are sitting filled with the color you have chosen.

Breathe deeply in and out and relax, inhaling the color in the pyramid. Breathe out those feelings in your body that you no longer want to feel. See those feelings leave your body as you exhale, or breathe out.

See how much better you feel? Pay attention. Notice how the feeling that you wanted to get rid of has now gone away. See how you now have a new, more positive feeling in your body.

COLORS THAT HELP CHANGE FEELINGS

THE COLOR	UNWANTED FEELING	GOOD FEELING
RED	Tired, no energy Sad	Energetic and strong Happy
ORANGE	Insecure Doubtful	Courageous Self-confident
YELLOW	Afraid, uptight	Happy, eager to do things
GREEN	Jealous or selfish Out of balance	Healing to the body Balanced
BLUE	Nervous Restless	Peaceful Quiet and serene
INDIGO (dark blue)	Indecisive Blocked	Aware and alert Open to intuition for information
VIOLET	Bored Spiritual growth stuck	More creative Closer to God-Source
WHITE	Scared, confused (all unwanted feelings, as white is all colors)	Protected, pure (all good feelings, as white is all colors)

See the little girl in the pyramid? She has just gotten rid of all the unwanted feelings in her body by using the colored pyramid meditation. You can, too!

LET'S MAKE A MEDITATION MANDALA

There is another easy way you can use color in your meditation and have a lot of fun in the process.

Have you ever made a meditation mandala? A mandala is a picture, an image, a collage of colored paper, symbols, shapes and the like in a geometric design. You can choose whatever you wish in creating your very own mandala.

EXERCISE

First, you need to have a large piece of white paper. Posterboard is even better because it is very sturdy, allowing you to hang it on your wall or set it against your dresser, bed, wall, chair and the like. You can make this mandala any size you wish – from, say, 81/2 by 11 inches to maybe 24 by 36 inches. Size is not important.

Now buy some colored construction paper. You can often buy several different colors in one package — red, orange, green, blue, yellow, navy blue or purple, black, brown, gray, white and pink.

As you begin making your very own mandala, think about the colors you like best. Choose these colors from the package of construction paper.

Now carefully cut different shapes from the construction paper. You can make circles, hearts, triangles, squares, stop-sign shapes, long, skinny shapes, new moons, stars, flowers, leaves and so forth. Cut any shape you feel like making.

Use stick glue or Elmer's white glue and carefully begin at the center of your poster board with a shape. Add different shapes from the center, moving outward in a circle or spiral. You can fill either the entire board or just a small portion of it. This is your mandala.

Once you have completed the mandala, set it up in a quiet part of your home or your room and begin your meditation by staring at your beautiful mandala. Each of the colors in your picture will be absorbed into your body for balance and healing.

2 • ENERGY AND OUR BODIES

WHAT IS ENERGY?

There are different types of energy that you are now going to learn about. First, there is physical energy, which you can sense with your eyes, ears, nose, mouth and body. Second, there is psychic (nonphysical) energy — energy that we know exists but cannot readily sense with our physical senses. Third, there is primal energy — that energy which emanates from God, the highest vibration of all.

Can you name some types of physical energy?

Energy comes from water, steam, sunlight, lightning, electricity and many other sources.

What does energy do? Energy runs machinery and power plants. Energy also helps human beings, animals and plants stay alive.

Energy comes from the air we breathe, the food we eat, the water we drink and from sunlight. The energy that comes into our bodies as we breathe is called our *life force.* It is the energy that keeps our bodies operating well, the energy that keeps our bodies alive.

ENERGY AND OUR CHAKRAS

Our life-force energy enters our body through seven very special energy centers called *chakras.* They can be seen with our mind's eye as different-colored spinning lights in the front of our bodies along our center. They can also be felt with our hands as whirlpools of energy, heat or tingling sensations.

The first center is called our *root chakra.* It is located at the end of our spine. Its color is red.

The second center, or *hara,* is located halfway between our bellybutton and the end of the spine. Its color is orange.

The third center is in our *solar plexus,* or belly button, and its color is yellow. This is the center where all our energy comes into our body from the universe around us. This is the center that sends the energy throughout the rest of our body to keep us happy and healthy.

The fourth center is located where our heart is and is called our *heart center.* It is colored green. This center is where we feel things such as love, happiness, sadness, anger and the like.

The fifth center is located in our throat area. Its color is light blue. This center helps us talk to each other and to our guardian angel. It is called our *throat chakra.*

The sixth center is located in the middle of our forehead between our eyebrows and is called the *third eye,* or *mind's eye.* Its color is dark blue or indigo. This center helps us sense energy that we are unable to see, feel, hear, smell or taste without our physical senses.

The seventh center is located at the top of our head. Its color is white or violet. It helps us connect with God to ask for help with things that bother us, to heal ourselves and others, and to become more aware of the world around us. It is called the *crown chakra*.

You can feel the chakra centers as they move.

EXERCISE TO FEEL AND SEE CHAKRAS

Rub your hands together until they get very warm and tingly. Place one hand, palm open toward your body. Hold your palm in front of each chakra center until you feel the energy there. Does all the energy in your chakras feel the same strength? If not, your chakras are not in balance (the energy coming in and out is not even), which can affect the way you feel.

You can feel the energy in another person's chakras as well. Rub the palms of your hands together until warm and tingly. Hold one hand out with the palm side facing the other person's stomach and chest area. Hold your hand over each of the seven chakras until you feel its energy. Is the energy the same in each center? Which centers feel stronger? What might that mean about how that person is feeling?

Stare at the chakra centers of another person. Can you see the swirling energy? Can you see the colors spinning? What colors do you see in each chakra?

Sometimes we feel our spine ache. This means that we have energy blocked in one of our chakra centers. We need to keep these centers open and unblocked so we can stay calm, energized and healthy.

EXERCISE TO BALANCE THE CHAKRAS

To balance your chakras, take your left hand with your thumb and index finger and gently pinch your nostrils closed. Then lift up the thumb and breathe in through your nose to the count of 6. Pinch your nostrils closed and count to 6. Then lift your index (pointer) finger and exhale to the count of 6. Pinch your nose closed and count to 6 again. Then lift your thumb and exhale while counting to 6. Repeat this exercise 5 times.

Do you feel more calm, relaxed and centered in your body?

You can count more quickly, or have fewer counts if you have trouble holding your breath to the count of 6.

OUR SEVEN ENERGY CENTERS — THE CHAKRAS

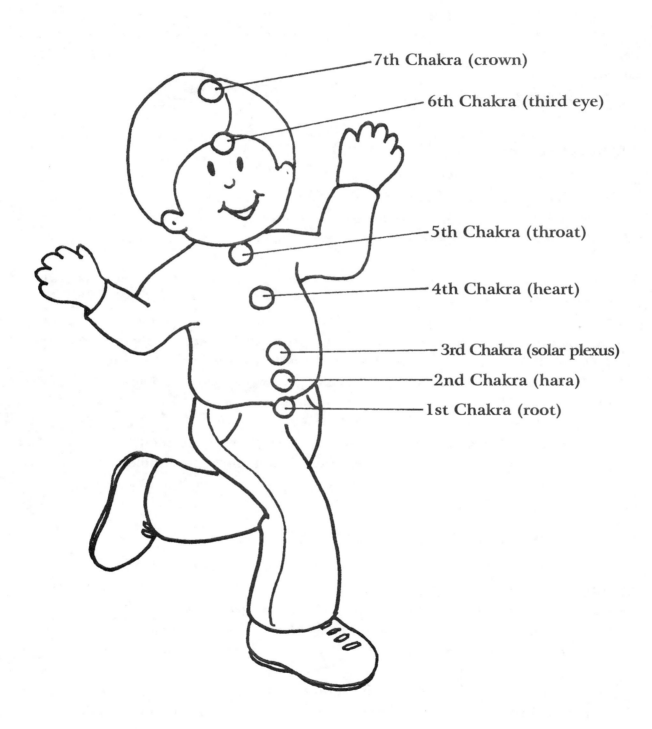

7th Chakra (crown)

6th Chakra (third eye)

5th Chakra (throat)

4th Chakra (heart)

3rd Chakra (solar plexus)

2nd Chakra (hara)

1st Chakra (root)

Balancing your chakras with colored paper. Over one of your chakras lay a small piece of colored construction paper, the same color as that chakra. Leave the colored paper there for a few minutes. Now test the energy with your hands again. Does it feel more even now?

EXERCISE TO TRANSMIT CHAKRA COLORS

Have a friend or one of your parents or a brother or sister sit on the floor about two feet away from you. Each of you should sit with legs crossed in the lotus position. Relax your body and mind.

Choose one person to be the sender and the other the receiver. The sender should choose to send to the receiver either the color pink from the heart center, blue from the throat center, violet from the third eye, or a rainbow from the crown chakra. Send the energy with its color to the receiver.

The receiver should relax, and as soon as he or she knows the color and feels which chakra the energy is being directed to, tell the sender what center and color is involved.

Now trade places. The receiver becomes the sender and the sender becomes the receiver.

Please note: Some people are very good at sending and others at receiving. Not everyone can do both jobs really well. Just try your best and have fun with this exercise.

OUR BODY'S ENERGY FIELD

Our body has an energy field around it called our *aura*. The aura is made up of four basic parts.

First, there is the *physical body* — that part of our body which we can see and sense with our physical senses.

Second is the *etheric,* or *emotional body*. This is the part of our aura that contains the colors you can see, the colors that show up in the Kirlian photographs you may have seen. This is the body in which our chakras are located. This body extends 6 to 8 inches from our physical body and is made up of our emotions — happiness, sadness, joy, anger, peacefulness and so on.

Third is the *mental body,* which is made up of our thoughts and feelings. It is magnetic energy.

Fourth is the *spiritual body*. This is the body that is directly connected to God. It extends from our physical body about 25 feet.

Everything has an aura — people, animals, plants, our houses, cars, toys, food products and so on. You can see these auras as colored lights on the outside of the body or whatever you are looking at.

THE HUMAN AURA

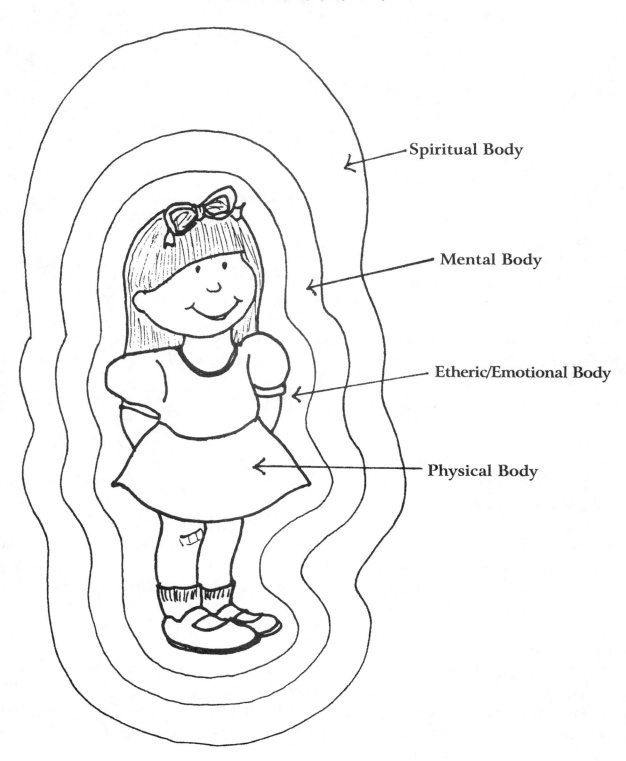

Spiritual Body

Mental Body

Etheric/Emotional Body

Physical Body

When you look at the aura you will see one color or a band of colors that represents a person's emotions, which are reflected in the aura by the chakra energy centers. Each of the colors you see tells you something about that person — what they are feeling or experiencing at the moment. You will find the colors changing as the person's feelings change.

WHAT DO THE COLORS MEAN?

Red in the aura means the person has a lot of energy. If the color is very dark, the person might be angry. Here is where it is important to use your feelings as well.

Orange tells you the person is very artistic or creative. This color could also mean the person has a lot of energy, a lot of courage (is very brave).

Yellow means the person is very bright and has a warm, friendly and happy personality.

Green tells you the person is very balanced and is able to do healing work for others.

Pink shows you the person is very loving and kind.

Blue means the person is very calm, very peaceful.

Purple tells you the person is very psychic and spiritual.

White is the color of a very, very spiritual or enlightened person.

SENSING THE AURA

You can feel the aura on your own body and the bodies of other people.

EXERCISE TO SENSE THE AURA

Rub the palms of your hands together until they are warm and tingly. Very slowly move one or both hands from about a foot away to about 6 to 8 inches from your physical body (don't touch it) until you feel a kind of pressure. This is the edge of your etheric body or your aura.

Another way to find the auric field is to have a friend stand across the room from you. Walk slowly toward your friend, who will keep his or her eyes closed. Ask your friend to say "stop" when he/she feels your energy.

You will have walked into the edge, or the beginning, of your friend's auric field — what we call his or her "space."

You can also sense the aura using *dowsing rods* that you can make at home with perhaps a little help from your mother or father. Although it takes practice, people for centuries have used a form of dowsing rods or forked branches to locate lost objects, underground water for digging wells, and buried objects like ancient pottery, arrowheads and so on.

MAKING DOWSING RODS

Take two pieces of wire about 16 inches long, with about 3 inches of that length bent in a 90-degree angle to form a handle. If you use a coat hanger for the wire, you will need two of them.

You will make two so you can hold one in each hand. You will hold the shorter end of the wires like this:

Hold them loosely so the wire can swing back and forth easily in your hands.

Now have a friend or your parent stand several feet away from you. As you approach your friend, holding the wires so the long ends are pointed toward him or her, the two wires will cross like an X when you have reached the edge of his or her aura, as shown below. (You need not hold your arms far apart, as in the drawing.)

When people protect themselves from energy that does not feel good, they will, without thinking about it, pull their energy closer to their body. When they feel good and trusting and are comfortable with the energy around them, their aura will extend farther away from their body.

SEEING THE AURA

Have a friend stand against a dark color such as a drapery or a door or even a blank wall. Look at the space beside his/her head and shoulders with your eyes halfway closed. Or you can focus your eyes on an invisible point several feet in front of the person. This should give you an unfocused view just like daydreaming gives you. See if a light background makes it easier to see the aura than a dark one.

You will begin to see colors. You may see one color, or many colors. The colors may stay the same or change as your friend's emotions change, right before your very eyes. For example, if he or she is feeling angry, you might see red. If your friend begins to feel very happy, you will see a lot of yellow.

When your friend first stands against the drapery or door, what colors do you see?

Ask your friend to feel happy. What colors do you see now?

Now ask your friend to feel angry about something. What change do you see now in the aura's colors?

From the description of what the colors mean, described on page 15, what can you tell about your friend's feelings?

Color this picture to reflect what you have seen in your friend's aura.

3 • WORKING WITH ENERGY

OUR FIVE SENSES — PHYSICAL BODY

OUR SIXTH SENSE (INTUITION) — NONPHYSICAL BODY

OUR FIVE SENSES VS. OUR INTUITION

Each of us uses five very important senses every day of our lives. Can you name the five senses?

1. We see with our eyes.
2. We hear with our ears.
3. We feel with our hands and bodies.
4. We taste with our mouth and tongue.
5. We smell with our nose.

Can you imagine how it would feel if you didn't have eyes to see with, if you were blind?

Can you imagine how it would be if you could not hear or feel or smell or taste?

How would you sense the world around you if you could not see, hear, feel, taste or smell?

Well, let's see just how you could do that. We will do a very special meditation where we shut off these five senses so you can see what senses are left, if any.

MEDITATION TO EXPERIENCE OUR SENSES

Sit or lie down with your spine very straight. Begin to breathe very deeply and begin to relax your whole body from the tip of your toes to the top of your head.

Now concentrate on your center. Concentrate on the bright light you see there as you close your eyes. Imagine you have never seen anything before. Pretend that you came into this world without sight, that you were born blind, that you have never seen your parents, your house, colors, people, plants, animals — that you have never seen the Sun or Moon or the stars . . . nothing. How do you feel?

Now imagine that you can't hear anything. Put your hands over your ears if you like. Bring all the sounds on the outside or inside of your head directly into your center . . . be very, very still.

Now imagine that you have never touched or felt anything with your hands or body ever before. Pretend that all of your feeling is located within your center. Imagine that you have never touched your body, the floor or walls, your toys, your mom or dad. If you have never touched or felt anything, how do you know anything is out there in the world?

Now imagine that you cannot taste anything and you've never tasted anything ever before. How do you feel, since you can't taste anything? How do you know what you are putting in your mouth?

Imagine that you can't smell anything, that you have never smelled cookies baking in the oven or flowers blooming in your yard. How do you feel, since you cannot smell anything?

All of your senses have disappeared into your center. Be very quiet. What do you have left?

Now we will bring back our five senses — one at a time. First let's smell the air in this room. How does it smell?

Let's taste our mouth. We have put the taste back into our mouth.

Let your ears listen to every sound in the room or outside. What do you hear?

Move around in your body. Feel your body with your hands. Feel the chair, the floor, the wall.

Now finally open your eyes and look around at the colors and objects in your room. What do you see?

You have learned from this meditation how it feels to turn off your five senses and sense with the *real* you that is more than just the senses of seeing, hearing, feeling, tasting and smelling.

The real you is inside of you. This is your center. The center is where we connect with the Source — God. It is a part of you that is really love, light and energy.

The real you does not need physical eyes, ears, hands, nose and mouth. The real you is able to *sense* things all around you in your world, without using your eyes, ears, hands, nose and mouth. This part of you is your sixth sense, your *intuition*.

WHAT IS INTUITION?

Intuition is the feeling inside of you that comes from your center, the source. When you turn off your other five senses, you see, feel, hear, taste and smell with your sixth sense, or your intuitive sense. You experience these senses in a different way — by sensing the energy that comes into your body through your energy centers. You "see," "hear," "feel," "taste" and "smell" nonphysical energy, or energy that is not easily visible to us. It is also called *psychic energy*.

You use your intuition when you get real quiet and sense the nonphysical energy through your energy centers or chakras. You can get very quiet in meditation and go inside to the source for answers to your questions and problems.

You have been using your intuition since you were first born even though you may not even realize you are using it. I am going to show you several ways in which you are using your intuition every day of your life.

- If you have to choose between two types of toys, sometimes you get a feeling about which one you should buy. This is your intuition helping you pick the right toy for you.
- Perhaps you have walked into a store and had a feeling that someone around you is not a very nice person. Your intuition is coming to you as a *feeling*, as a warning to keep you safe.
- Have you ever had a dream about something that actually came true days, weeks

or even months later? This is a very special kind of dream that sends you a message and picture about something that is about to take place in your life. The dream helps you be prepared to handle the event. This type of dream is called a *precognitive dream*. (Precognitive means knowing beforehand.)

- Do you see the angels around you, or little balls of colored lights, or special "friends," as you call them? And only you can see them and talk to them? These special friends are your *spirit guides* or *guardian angels* who come with you when you are born to help guide you, protect you and work with you when you have a problem or are feeling lonely. They are always with you. All you have to do is ask them to be with you and help you with problems or other things that you need help with. Seeing these special friends is a very important part of your intuitive abilities. It is called *clairvoyance*, or seeing with your mind's eye.

- Can you hear your spirit friends talking to you? Have you ever heard your name softly called, a soft knocking in your room, or other sounds around you when no physical person is near? This is a special part of your intuitive abilities known as *clairaudience*.

- Do you sometimes know what people are going to say before they say the words? Do you sometimes know who is at the door before you open it? Or who is calling before you pick up the telephone? This is called *mental telepathy* — sending and receiving energy as thoughts.

- Do you sometimes feel like you are flying? Do you ever feel like you are up at the ceiling, floating around outside, or that you can look down at yourself sleeping in your bed or playing in your room? This is a very natural experience called an *out-of-body experience*. This happens when your etheric/emotional body, which is a part of your aura, separates from your physical body, allowing it to move about freely.

Your etheric/emotional body is very light. It has a different form. You can still see, hear, feel, taste and smell, but in a different way. When you are traveling in this way, you can move about very freely and quickly. This part of you always returns to your physical body unless it is time for you to pass over in death. Then you travel on to the Source and live in the spirit world until it is time for you to return to Earth for another lifetime. You live in a very beautiful, peaceful world with God and the angels.

INTUITION WORKSHEET

Write down those experiences when you have used your intuition. Then you can see that you are already using your intuition in more ways than you may realize.

How I am using my intuition in feeling things:

1. _____
2. _____
3. _____

How I am using my intuition as seeing or clairvoyance:

1. _____
2. _____
3. _____

What precognitive dreams I have had (dreams that come true):

1. _____
2. _____
3. _____

How I have used my clairaudient abilities in listening to the spirit world:

1. _____
2. _____
3. _____

How I have used mental telepathy, or sent and received thoughts:

1. _____
2. _____
3. _____

How I have experienced myself out of body, in my etheric/emotional body:

1. _____
2. _____
3. _____

WORKING WITH ENERGY

There are many different ways in which you can work with the energy that you cannot sense with your five physical senses, that energy we call nonphysical (psychic) energy.

It is much easier to sense this nonphysical energy when we are calm, relaxed and focused. Therefore, the first step we must take is to center our own energy using the following exercises.

CENTERING MEDITATION

By centering our energy we are simply concentrating our mind on our heart center or our solar plexus center while breathing very deeply in relaxed, continuous breaths.

Imagine that you are like a giant scoop. As you breathe and concentrate on your center, you reach out into the universe and scoop back into your center all the energy you've scattered as you've worked and played during the day. As you bring your energy back, you begin to feel very calm and relaxed, like your whole body is in a straight line. And you are better able to concentrate on the energy you cannot sense with your five senses.

GROUNDING MEDITATION

Grounding our energy means that we connect our physical, emotional, mental and spiritual bodies with the energy of the Earth beneath our feet, and with the Source, or God, above us. When we ground ourselves, we have a better feeling of balance in our bodies. We do not feel spaced out. We can focus and concentrate better on our work at school and our play with the energy games in this workbook.

To ground, pretend that you are a tree. Your feet are the roots, your body the trunk, and your arms, hands and head are the branches and top of the tree. Imagine your roots growing deeper and deeper into the ground, holding you very firmly to the ground under your feet. Keep breathing very deeply as you do this. Then imagine the top of your head opening up and letting pure white light come down into your body, mixing with the Earth energy. The Earth energy feels very warm and tingly. The white-light energy makes you feel pure, strong and powerful.

THE WHITE BUBBLE OF PROTECTION

Our bodies are like little television receivers. When a feeling or thought is sent out in the form of energy, we can receive this energy in the form of a thought or feeling in our body. The energy from other people comes in through our chakras, or energy centers.

If the energy from other people is angry or sad, we may begin to feel angry or sad ourselves. If it is happy, loving energy, we may begin to feel the same way — happy and loving.

We need to protect ourselves from other people's energy when they are feeling bad so we don't feel bad, too. To protect ourselves from other people's thoughts and feelings that we don't want, we can create the protective bubble.

After centering and grounding, imagine drawing down a beam of white light from God and into the top of your head, then out your heart chakra. Imagine that you are completely surrounded in a beautiful white bubble of light that protects you from any unpleasant feelings that you might otherwise feel.

You can create this protection whenever you are afraid. It will help you get rid of your fears.

LEARNING TO FOCUS

What does it mean to focus on something, to concentrate?

What happens when we think about too many things at one time?

Right. We start to get scattered. We don't know what to think about or do first. We get too many thoughts in our head at one time and it keeps us from getting things done.

When we learn to focus and concentrate on one thing at a time, we are better able to

- *Quiet our mind.*
- *Get more relaxed.*
- *Go deeper into our source, or center.*
- *Become more sensitive and aware of everything around us.*
- *Become more sensitive and aware of nonphysical energy.*

One of the easiest ways to learn to focus on one thing at a time is to meditate on a candle flame.

FOCUSING EXERCISE

Gaze at the candle's flame for as long as is comfortable (5 to 10 minutes if possible). Then close your eyes, holding the image of the flame in your mind as long as you can. It may move around in your head. Try to hold the image in the center of your forehead. When it moves, bring it back to the center of your forehead. Pay close attention to the colors that you see.

What colors did you see?

Did you see any images? If so, what did you see?

Draw one or more pictures in a notebook of what you saw in the candle flame. Color the candle flame in the drawing the same colors you saw when you closed your eyes, the colors that appeared in your mind's eye as you watched the flame with your eyes closed.

The more you practice focusing and concentrating, the better able you will be to quiet your mind and see, hear, feel, taste and smell the nonphysical energy around you.

FEELING THE ENERGY IN OBJECTS (PSYCHOMETRY)

Everything around you has energy — plants, rocks, animals, people.

One way to do a psychic reading for another person is to hold an object that was worn by them, such as a piece of jewelry, a watch or clothing. This is called *psychometry*.

There are many great psychics in the world who work with police departments, helping to solve crimes the police cannot solve. The psychics hold objects found at the scene of the crime and read the energy from the objects. The psychics can tell all about the crime — the person who committed it, the victim, what happened before and after the crime, where the criminal went. This is not something only a few great psychics can do. You can read energy in objects, too. We all can.

PERSONAL OBJECTS

You can hold a piece of jewelry or clothing and read the energy of the item, telling all about the person who has worn it the most — their hair and eye color, whether they are male or female, married or single, whether they have children and if so, how many, what their ages are and so on. You can sense where they live, what type of work they do, and all about their personality — what type of person they are.

PSYCHOMETRY MEDITATION

Get very quiet. Relax your body and breathe very deeply. Concentrate on your center and let your mind be empty. Now pick up a piece of clothing or jewelry that you know nothing about. Have your mom, dad or a friend help you. Let the feelings and thoughts come into your mind. Say the first thing that comes into your mind. Don't try to change the thoughts, because what comes to you right away (in the first 30 seconds) is always correct. Say it. This is not a test like in school.

What do you feel?
What do you see?
Can you describe the person who has worn this item the most?
What color is their hair and eyes? Married or single?
How many children do they have, if any?
Where do they live?
Where do they work?
What type of person is he/she? Happy? Sad? Busy? Peaceful? Young? Old?
Did this person buy this item for him/herself or was it a gift?

PHOTOGRAPHS

You can hold a photograph and read all about the event that was taking place when the picture was taken, all about the people in the picture, what they are doing, feeling, and their past, present and future. You can even tell what time of year the photo was taken and what the weather was like.

LEARNING TO FEEL COLORS

Here is a fun way to practice feeling or sensing energy in objects through working with colors. Remember: The more you practice, the easier it will be to read the energy in any object you touch.

COLORS MEDITATION

You will need the following items to make your cards: (1) 3 x 5 index cards, (2) at least 7 different colors of construction paper, and (3) stick glue, Elmer's glue or scotch tape.

Fold the index card in half. On one half of the card, glue or tape a small piece of colored construction paper. You may cut the colored paper into any shape – a triangle, square, circle, whatever.

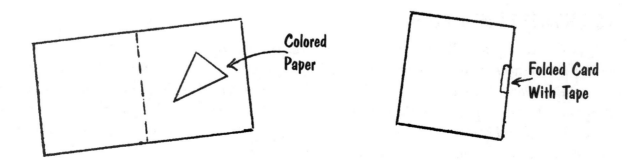

Colored Paper

Folded Card With Tape

Fold the other half of the index card over the colored paper and tape the edges together if necessary (so you can't peek).

Mix up the cards after you complete the gluing or taping of several different samples. Close your eyes and pick one. Hold the card between the palms of your hands and let the colored image come into your inner vision through your third eye. What color do you see, know or sense?

Ask your mom, dad or friend to help you select a photograph that you know nothing about. They can help you in your work by telling you when you have received correct information about the people or the situation photographed.

Get very quiet and relax your body by breathing very deeply. Concentrate on your center. Now pick up the photograph between the palms of your hands. Let thoughts just flow into your empty mind. Say the first thing that comes into your mind. Don't try to change what you receive. Psychic information comes in an instant. Just say what you see, hear or know.

What do you see?

What do you feel?

What time of year was the picture taken? Was it a holiday?

What was the weather like when the photo was taken? Hot? Cold? Rainy? Windy? Sunny?

If there are people in the picture, are they related? Do they like having their picture taken?

What can you tell about the people in the picture? Are they happy people? Are they sad? What might happen to them in the future?

Practice with different items and photos belonging to friends and relatives. You will really surprise them with all the information you can give them from the items you hold in your hands. Now you are practicing *psychometry*.

DOWSING

You have lost your favorite toy. You are sure it is somewhere in the house . . . but where?

Did you know that you can find your toy just by closing your eyes and feeling its energy? Did you know that your toy's energy can lead you right to it? Let's give it a try

DOWSING MEDITATION

Have your parents or a friend hide one of your toys somewhere in your house. Don't peek!

Now close your eyes. Breathe deeply and relax your body. Let all the thoughts in your head flow right on through.

Concentrate on your toy. Let the feeling of the toy come into your thoughts. Ask yourself: Is it in the kitchen . . . the bedroom . . . the living room? and so on. Suddenly there will be a feeling in your body, a very strong feeling, about a certain room. Go to that room.

Clear your mind. Breathe deeply. Relax your body. Concentrate only on your toy. Is it to my left? My right? In front of me or behind me?

Wait for a feeling about the direction. Your body will tell you which direction to look.

Once you find the direction, keep your eyes closed and ask if the toy is higher or lower, on top of something or under something. Keep asking these questions until you know right where it is.

Another way to find it is to hold your hands palms outward and walk around the area until you feel a warmth or coolness of energy.

Practice this technique until you are comfortable that you can find any lost object with ease. Try this exercise the next time someone you know loses something. You will be the hero of the day. And it's easy.

SENDING AND RECEIVING THOUGHTS (TELEPATHY)

You have probably already practiced this technique without even realizing it. How many times have you known what someone was going to say before they ever said it, and you were right? This is known as *mental telepathy* — sending and receiving non-physical energy.

TELEPATHY MEDITATION

Have a friend sit on the floor about two feet away from you. One of you will send the message and the other will receive it. After you have chosen who will send and who will receive, have the sender pick a color of the rainbow — red, orange, yellow, green, blue or violet.

The receiver needs to be very quiet, without any thoughts at all. Close your eyes. The sender should think about only the color . . . spell it, say it and imagine it in your mind.

Wait until the receiver names the color. As soon as the receiver picks up a color, he/she should say what color it is. Remember, it is okay to get a "wrong" color. Keep trying. You will be surprised at how soon you can feel and know every color correctly.

Now trade places. The sender is the receiver and the receiver is the sender. Try sending colors, numbers, shapes, pictures of your favorite fruits and vegetables, animals, letters of the alphabet.

Try sending chakra energy with the color of the chakra you learned about in the previous chapter. For example, if you wish to send energy from your heart chakra, send the color green or pink and a warm, loving energy from your heart to the other person's heart. See if they can feel the energy and see the color. Trade places. Try the heart, throat and third eye chakras. See what happens.

HEARING (CLAIRAUDIENCE)

Sometimes when you are about to go to sleep at night or awaken in the morning you may inwardly hear your name softly called, the telephone ringing, doors closing and other sounds. These are the sounds of our spirit guides, or guardian angels, letting us know they are near to help and protect us.

We can learn to hear them even better by practicing being quiet, by listening very, very carefully.

CLAIRAUDIENCE MEDITATION

Get very quiet. Close your eyes. Breathe very deeply.

Let your body relax completely and let your mind become as still as you can possibly make it. (It is best to choose a room that is very quiet and away from the noise outside, the front door, the phone and other people in your house.)

Listen. Listen . . . listen . . . listen!

Listen to all the sounds in the room.

Don't focus your mind on any thought.

Listen to the different sounds.

Now open your eyes and write down the sounds that you heard. Write them on a piece of paper so you can keep a record of what you hear.

Now go outside. Sit quietly. Close your eyes.

Let your mind get very still. Listen carefully to all the sounds you hear outside.

Write down the sounds you hear on your piece of paper.

It is also a good idea to keep a pencil and paper next to your bed. Then you can write down the things you hear just before you go to sleep and just as you awaken in the morning. What do you hear? Shhh! Listen very carefully!

DEVELOPING THE SKILLS OF
CLAIRVOYANCE AND TELEPATHY

This is a very special game you can play at home to help you develop your clairvoyance (ability to see with your mind's eye) and your mental telepathy (sending and receiving thoughts).

For this exercise you will need white index cards and a light blue or yellow pencil, a light color that would not show through the back of the card when it is upside down.

CARD EXERCISE

With your colored pencil and five index cards, draw the symbols, each one on a separate card. Make two sets, one for you and one for your partner.

Have your partner mix up his/her five cards and lay them face down on the table or floor so you cannot see the symbols.

Now take a few very deep breaths, relax your entire body, and let all thoughts flow out of your mind, concentrating only on the cards your partner has laid down.

Lay your own cards down in the same order (first to last) as your partner did, but place them face up, making sure they are in the order you want them, according to the energy you have picked up, felt or seen from your partner's cards. Then ask your partner to turn his/her cards face up one at a time.

Keep a record of how many cards you get right each time you do the exercise. Take turns tuning in to the other person's cards and trying to match them exactly.

Each time you do the exercise you will find that you are correct more often than not. You do have to concentrate. Do not change the cards once you have placed them on the floor. We are usually right the very first time, and when we change the card order, we end up with an incorrect match.

4 • LEARNING TO PROTECT OURSELF FROM NEGATIVE ENERGIES

POSITIVE VS. NEGATIVE ENERGIES

When we speak of feelings, we often talk about positive feelings and negative feelings. Positive feelings are feelings that make us feel good, such as loving, happy feelings. Negative feelings are feelings that make us feel uncomfortable, such as sad, unhappy, nervous feelings.

Can you think of some positive feelings you have about yourself?

1. _____
2. _____
3. _____

Can you think of some negative feelings you have about yourself?

1. _____
2. _____
3. _____

FEELINGS MEDITATION

Close your eyes. Breathe deeply and relax your body. Go deep inside your body, into every finger and toe, into every tiny little part of your body.

What kinds of feelings are hiding inside your body?

Are they happy, loving feelings?

Are they unhappy, sad, angry feelings?

Which are positive feelings? Which are negative feelings?

Find someone to help you with this next part of the exercise.

Close your eyes. Now center yourself in your body and relax from the tips of your toes to the top of your head. Ask your partner to think about an emotion —anger, joy, sadness, happiness and so on. Let your body feel the kind of energy your partner is sending out. How do you feel?

When you are at school, what are some of the feelings you get from people around you?

How do other people's feelings make you feel?

What feelings do you get when you are in a large crowd of people such as those at the state fair, Disneyland, your park or playground, and so on?

What kind of feelings do you pick up in your own home?

These feelings come into our bodies as nonphysical (psychic) energy. This energy enters our chakra centers. Where does the energy come in? Do you remember which chakra is responsible?

Many of us are too open. This means we are extra sensitive to psychic energy. We feel everything going on around us — what others are thinking or feeling. This can be positive or negative energy, depending on how the other person is feeling.

We do not want to be affected by negative energy, so we use what we call *psychic protection* to keep away from us energy that does not belong in our auric space.

WAYS TO CREATE PROTECTION

How do you protect yourself now from unwanted energy? We are going to learn some methods to protect us from negative energy.

Some of these methods you may already be aware of, or perhaps they will be new to you. Choose the method that works best for you. None are better than others. They all work equally well.

CLEARING THE AURA

Stand with your hands crossed in front of your body, arms downward. Count to four. Keeping your hands crossed over each other, raise your arms over your head as high as you can reach while you hold your breath and count to 16. Then lower your hands to the count of 8.

Repeat the exercise at least 3 times. The more counting you do, the more protected you will feel.

BUBBLE OF LIGHT

Sit quietly. Breathe very deeply and close your eyes. Imagine the top of your head opening and God's white light coming down through the top of your head and out your heart center.

Imagine yourself being wrapped in a cocoon or bubble of white light, until your whole body is wrapped in white light.

CRYSTAL–LASER WAND

For this exercise you will need a crystal laser wand. This is a special type of crystal that is long and pointed.

Hold the crystal in both hands. Point the crystal toward the floor. Draw an imaginary line all around your body with the laser wand. Is it really imaginary?

Have someone reach out and feel the energy you have just placed around your body. What does he/she feel?

TOWER OF LIGHT MEDITATION

Breathe deeply. Relax your body and stand up straight. Imagine a blue light all around you.

Now imagine a ball of brilliant white light above your head. This light is coming from your higher self, your spiritual self. Imagine white light coming down like fairy dust and mixing with the blue light. Imagine that this is God's light protecting you from all negative energy.

Slowly open your eyes, knowing that the blue-and-silver light is still protecting you for as long as you want it to.

GUARDIAN ANGEL MEDITATION

Ask your guardian angel to come into your auric space and be with you for protection and guidance.

CRYSTALS AND STONES

You can wear or carry crystals and stones to strengthen your aura, thus protecting yourself from any negative energy.

The crystals and stones will let you stay open, but will not allow you to take on negative energy into your body. The crystals and stones will also help you change negative feelings to positive feelings, thereby making you feel happy and not worried or afraid.

The best stones to work with for protection are:

- Turquoise (it strengthens the entire body)
- Clear quartz
- Jade
- Amber
- Citrine
- Black Tourmaline
- Obsidian
- Hematite

i am helpful ☺

5 • RELEASING UNWANTED THOUGHTS AND FEELINGS: CREATING AND USING AFFIRMATIONS

i love myself ♡

i am loved ✿♡♡✿✿

WHAT ARE ENERGY BLOCKS?

Energy blocks are created by our thoughts and feelings and represent stuck emotions that move into our chakra centers and can't get out until we become aware of them and release them. Energy blocks can feel like a big, thick cloud in one of our chakras, and can also show up in other parts of our body, such as elbows, knees, head, neck and so on. These blocks can make us feel stuck, unable to move forward in our lives.

When you pass your hand over the edge of the aura, as you learned in a previous section, you can actually become aware of a block as a hot or cold spot, or a thickness in the energy. You may also see a grayish cloud with your third-eye vision in the area in which the block occurs.

In this section you will learn how to examine your body and chakra system for energy blocks and then learn how to release those blocks.

WHERE DO BLOCKS ORIGINATE?

Many of our emotional blocks begin in childhood, even from the moment of birth. Many of us are still living with ideas presented to us by our family, friends, teachers and the society in which we live.

You may have heard the statements, "Boys don't cry" or "Girls don't climb trees," or "Act like a lady" or "Men always have to provide for their families." These statements are called *limiting beliefs*. They make us think we have to act in certain ways — that we cannot be ourselves, be who we really are. These beliefs block energy.

When we are little, we learn how to feel about ourselves and about life in general from the adults around us. If you grow up with people who are always unhappy or frightened, or who feel guilty or angry, that is how you begin to feel the same way as those adults. That is how you learn about negative things in your world and in yourself. How many times have you heard these statements? "You can never do anything right." "It's all your fault." "If you get angry, you're a bad person." "You should have been a boy instead of a girl" — or — "You should have been a girl instead of a boy."

As you grow up, you create the same kind of emotional environment that you remember from your early home life. And when you have a relationship with a man or woman as you get older, you tend to treat that person as you were treated by your mom or dad.

And sometimes we even treat ourselves just like our parents treat us. We scold and punish ourselves, saying to ourselves, "Gee, I never do anything right." "It's all my fault." "I am so stupid." These are negative statements. On the other hand, do you ever hear yourself think, "I am so beautiful, so wonderful" or "I love myself" because you hear your parents speak to you in that manner? These positive statements will certainly make a difference in your life, because you will not have the same type of energy blocks as those you have when negative thoughts are believed.

You can create a very loving, positive world for yourself by thinking positive thoughts.

What are you thinking about right now? Is it positive? Is it negative? Remember that what you are thinking at this very moment is something that is creating your future. If you think kind, loving, accepting thoughts about yourself and others, this is the type of environment you will create for yourself.

If you are catching yourself thinking a negative thought at any time during the day, stop and say, "Cancel, cancel, cancel," and then change the negative thought to a positive one. For example, if you are thinking to yourself, "I can't do anything right," stop right there and say, "I do everything right." This unlocks the negative thought. You will find your day and your whole life flowing much more smoothly as you keep catching these negative thoughts and your life will be much happier as your thinking begins to change.

CHANGING BELIEF SYSTEMS BY USING POSITIVE AFFIRMATIONS

An affirmation is a positive statement that you create for yourself and say to yourself in order to make things better in your life. When making affirmations:

1. Write and say them as if they already exist. For example, "I *have* straight A's on my report card," not "I *will get* straight A's on my report card." When you say, "I will," you are expecting to receive what you ask for someday in the future — and you certainly don't want to wait for good things to happen in your life, do you? Besides, each day is always *now*.

2. Write them in a positive way. Avoid using negative words when writing affirmations. For example, do not say, "I don't want bad grades." Instead, write, "I always make good grades in school."

MAKING AN AFFIRMATION CHART

It is always easier to stay happy and think positively when we have something that reminds us to think that way. One way to remind ourselves to catch negative thoughts and think happy, positive thoughts is by having an affirmation chart on the wall.

To make your chart you will need:

1. A large piece of paper, 11 x 17 inches, or poster board.
2. Marking pens, either black or colored.
3. As many wonderful thoughts about yourself as you can imagine.

Now let's get started. Keep your affirmations short, simple and clear. The shorter the better, because then you won't feel like you have to work so hard in repeating or writing them.

Write affirmations that are right for you. You do not have to use other people's affirmations unless they are comfortable for you. It is always better to write your own. And if you wish, you can ask your parents and friends for ideas and assistance.

When you use affirmations you are creating something new, not trying to change something that already exists. Affirmations help you change your feelings and beliefs about yourself and your life in general, thereby helping you release energy blocks in your body.

Can you write down at least five affirmations for yourself?

Repeat them to yourself every morning and every night before you go to bed. Keep a record of what happens in your life when you say your affirmations. You will be surprised!

MY AFFIRMATION CHART . . .
1. I am loving and kind.
2. I am helpful.
3. I am healthy.
4. I am a beautiful, loving person.
5. God loves me and protects me.
6. God's light is my protection.
7. I am truthful.
8. I get good grades at school.
9. I have a lot of friends who love me.
10.
11.
12.
13.
14.
15.
(Can you think of more great things to say about yourself? You can keep adding to your chart each day as feelings come into your mind. Try to fill up the entire chart with good, wonderful, positive things to say about you!)

RELEASING BLOCKED ENERGY FROM THE CHAKRAS

Each of your chakra centers is responsible for some form of sensing through your physical body. Each chakra is responsible for a different type of emotion or feeling.

The first (root) chakra is concerned with your needs to survive on planet Earth:
• a house to live in
• enough good, nourishing food to eat
• clothes to wear
• loving parents to take care of you.

It is also responsible for your feeling connected to the Earth. We call this being grounded. When you don't feel grounded you tend to be spaced out. Then it is hard to concentrate on schoolwork and other important duties.

The second chakra is concerned with
• your ability to feel energy on the outside of your body
• your feeling good about being a boy or a girl
• your ability to use creative energy, have new ideas, do inspired artwork, play music and so on.

The third chakra deals with
• your body's level of energy; you feel tired when it is blocked
• your personal power (not letting other people boss you or make you do things you don't want to do), and self confidence.

The fourth chakra deals with
• your emotions and touch
• healing hurtful childhood experiences.

The fifth chakra helps us
• hear our spirit guides and guardian angels
• communicate with our parents, teachers and friends.

The sixth chakra gives us the ability to
• see with our mind's eye, or spirit eye.

Sometimes we block it because we are afraid to see the future or see scary things about other people.

The seventh (crown) chakra helps us feel connected to God and feel one with God.

RELEASING BLOCKED ENERGY

*Now close your eyes. Put your attention on your **first (root) chakra**. You should see a bright red color there.*

If the color is muddy-looking or dark, or if you see or sense a cloud, there is an energy blockage in your root chakra. If that happens, ask your higher self what the blockage is about. The answer will come as a feeling, a thought, a picture – or you might even hear spoken words.

For instance, you might hear or feel: "You are afraid because you hear your parents fight all the time and you think they might get a divorce. What would happen to you then? Don't they love you?"

When you know what the blockage is about, go to work changing the picture. Write an affirmation such as, "My parents love me very much. My parents love each other very much. I feel strong and secure," and so on.

You could also send love to yourself and to your parents, or sit down and talk to them if you feel comfortable and tell them how you feel. They might be able to explain the situation in a way that will make you feel more comfortable.

*Now take your attention to your **second chakra** and see the color orange.*

If the color is dark or muddy or you sense a cloud, there is a blockage in your second chakra. Ask what the block is. It could be that you are not feeling very creative, that you are upset with yourself for not feeling creative or for not doing the kind of work you know you can do. Or perhaps your teacher told you that you should have done a much better job on your report.

Perhaps you feel that being a boy or being a girl is creating problems in your life. For example, you are a girl and you want to play baseball with your brother and his friends, but they tell you it's just for boys. Or as a boy you want to jump rope with your sister and her friends and they tell you it's not for boys, just girls.

Look at the block. Decide what the problem is. Make an affirmation to change the picture.

*Let's look at your **third chakra** and see the color yellow. Is the color a bright yellow? If not, ask what the blockage is.*

Perhaps you feel badly about letting a friend push you around or try to get you to do things you know are wrong or that you don't want to do.

Perhaps you have not been taking care of yourself and your energy level is low.

Once you know what the problem is, you can work to change the picture.

*In looking at your **fourth chakra**, look for a bright green. If the color is anything but bright green, there is a blockage to examine. Go inside and ask what the feeling or emotion is. Are you hurt, angry, sad? Do you feel guilty, ashamed of something you did or didn't do? What is the emotion?*

Once you know what emotion is blocking your heart chakra, you can release it through your breathing and by creating a positive energy with an affirmation.

*The **fifth chakra** is light blue or turquoise when clear. If you experience a cloudy feeling or dark color, there might be things you need to say but are afraid to, things that might hurt someone else's feelings, which you don't want to do.*

To help clear this type of energy blockage, imagine in front of you the person you want to speak to. Then say the words that are in your throat, either out loud or in your mind. Say anything and everything you want to express, allowing all the emotions to come out. When all of those energies are released, you will find loving feelings underneath. You need not physically face someone to tell them what is in your heart and mind. When you have completed this exercise, you might be surprised at how much better you feel and how the situation between you and that other person will improve. On the level we call the etheric, that person heard what you said to them.

*In examining the **sixth chakra**, look for dark blue or purple. If you feel or see a blockage here, it might be about not wanting to know about the future or about people you care about. Sometimes we might see a past life and not recognize that's what it is and be scared and confused. Once we are aware that seeing these things is a natural process to help us understand and grow, the blockage will disappear.*

One of the simplest affirmations to clear the sixth chakra is, "I am willing to see clearly on all levels."

*The **seventh** (crown) **chakra** represents our connection with God. It might be a bit muddy or be partly closed when we do not feel very loving and close to God. The more love we feel inside for ourselves and for everyone and everything in the universe, the more open and clear this chakra will be.*

USING SOUND TO CLEAR ENERGY BLOCKAGES

Each of your chakras can be opened and cleared by using a certain sound from your own voice or a certain note of the musical scale. If you are using your voice, you will take a deep breath and make the sound, letting it flow from your mouth for as long as you can. Repeat at least three times. You will feel the sound vibrate in the chakra center you are working on.

If you choose to use a piano or some other musical instrument, strike the note slowly at least three times, or until you feel the chakra is clear.

USING SOUND TO CLEAR BLOCKAGES

To clear each chakra by using sound, tone these syllables:

Root (1st) chakra — *eh* as in "red."

2nd chakra — *oh* as in "home."

3rd chakra — *ah-ooo-mmm.*

4th chakra — *ah.*

5th chakra — *oo* as in "blue.*"*

6th chakra — *ee* as in "bee."

Crown (7th) — *om* as in "home."

To clear your chakras by using musical notes, use the ascending scale below:

Root (1st) chakra — C

2nd chakra — D

3rd chakra — E

4th chakra — F sharp

5th chakra — G sharp

6th chakra — high A

Crown (7th) chakra — high B

To clear energy blockages with crystals and stones, see the last section of the chapter, Working with Crystals and Stones.

LOVING OURSELVES AND RELEASING UNWANTED FEELINGS

As we live our lives on planet Earth, it is important to feel good about ourselves and the other people who share the planet with us.

We want to build happy, joyful thoughts and experiences, not thoughts and experiences that make us feel unhappy. We want to treat other people just like we would want to be treated ourselves — in a happy, loving, joyful way.

There are many ways in which we can use thoughts of love to change the energy around us from unhappy, unloving energy to happy, loving energy.

As we meditate and go inside ourselves, we can receive help with our work in school. We can receive help in dealing with friends and family members at home.

For example, perhaps you are having a problem in school learning a particular subject. You can get very quiet and center yourself, go inside to your center and ask yourself to be open and receptive in school so you can learn more easily. Ask for help from your spirit guides and guardian angels to allow you to concentrate better on the subject you are having difficulty with.

If you are having a problem with your teacher or a parent, brother or sister, sit quietly and send that person love, silently asking your spirit guide or guardian angel to help you be more in tune with the person.

Anytime someone sends angry, unloving thoughts to you, close your eyes, center yourself and imagine a ring of pink flowers all around him or her. Send a pink beam of light from your heart to their heart. Keep sending the pink light until you feel that attitude about you has changed. You can really feel this change. You will notice a visible change in his/her attitude in a very short time after you start sending love.

Love is like a wave. It flows from one person to another. It brings the person giving the love and the person receiving the love closer together. Love brings you together so you think the same way — loving thoughts — instead of disagreeing or fighting with each other.

SENDING LOVE MEDITATION

Sit across from your partner. One of you should be the sender and the other the receiver. Choose the role you want to be first and then switch roles with the other person so each of you has a chance to play both parts.

The sender should send out a pink beam of light from his/her heart to the heart of the person receiving. With this beam of pink light, the sender should also send a feeling of love – strong love, the kind of love that says, "I love you no matter who you are. I love you no matter what you think or do. I love you no matter what you believe."

Ask the person receiving the love:

How did it feel?

Did you feel the energy in your heart?

Did you feel the love I sent?

Did you see the pink light I sent you?

Did it make you feel happy and loving?

Practice sending beautiful, loving thoughts to a friend. Send the feeling from your heart.

Practice sending love and the color pink to a friend, your parents and family, your teacher, or just out into the world to all the people everywhere.

Wouldn't it be wonderful if everyone in the whole world loved one another all of the time, unconditionally, no matter who they are, what they believe in, what they do, where they live and so on?

LOVING YOURSELF

Before you can really love other people, it is important that you first love yourself, *really* love yourself, just as you are.

Does that sound easy? Now, wait a minute. Do you really love yourself just as you are right now? Can you really be happy with the way you are without wishing you were shorter, taller, thinner, fatter, smarter, a different sex (a boy instead of a girl or a girl instead of a boy)? Can you really love yourself without wishing your hair or eyes were a different color, that you had more friends, a different personality?

Remember one thing: God created you just like Him/Herself. Since God is perfect and you are created to be just like God, then you too are already perfect now in every way.

You came into this world to learn a lesson and you chose the way you look and act to help you learn that lesson. Be happy about yourself, love yourself, and the world will think you are great. The whole world will love you right back.

Very often while growing up, different situations in our lives affect us emotionally.

Someone might call us stupid or make us feel bad about ourselves. Someone might say or do something that causes us to feel we are not good enough or that we are not loved. We might develop angry feelings toward someone because we feel that person treated us badly in some way or said something to us or about us that was not true. These feelings keep us from being the kind, loving person we can be.

But these feelings can be changed very easily to more happy, loving thoughts. We can do this changing through a process called *releasing*. Releasing thoughts and feelings that we no longer want is really a very easy process. All that is needed is a quiet place where we can use our breathing exercise.

RELEASING UNWANTED FEELINGS

Move to a part of your house where you will not be disturbed by people, pets, telephones or your friends knocking on the door. Lie down or sit in a chair. Get into a very relaxed position.

If you wish, before you get into your relaxed position, take a large piece of paper and write down the thoughts and feelings you want to get rid of. You can write one thought or feeling or as many as you feel inside your body.

Now think about a thought or feeling in your body that you no longer want. Think about a thought or feeling that seems to be stuck inside and is keeping you from thinking and acting in more happy, positive ways. These are usually thoughts of anger, sadness, frustration, guilt, feelings of being used by your friends. It could be a feeling that your parents don't really love or want you.

Beginning with the first thought or feeling that you wrote on your paper, use the following exercise to change it. You will get rid of one unwanted thought or feeling at a time until they are all gone.

As you release each unwanted thought or feeling, scratch those words from your paper. You can do one thought or feeling at a time, or spend some time in silence and get rid of all of them at once.

CREATING NEW FEELINGS AND THOUGHTS

To begin, relax your body from your toes up to the top of your head. Take deep, relaxed breaths. As you breathe in, think about the thought or feeling you wish to release. As you exhale, imagine that thought or feeling leaving your body.

Now think about some thought or feeling that you would like to put in your body to replace the old thought or feeling.

For example, if you want to get rid of anger at a friend for telling you that you are stupid, imagine the friend smiling at you and telling you how smart you are. Forgive him/her for saying you are stupid. Tell yourself that you are very smart. Believe that you are smart. Know that you are smart. After all, God is smart, and God created you just like Him/Her. Right?

Now, as you inhale, breathe in the wonderful feeling and thought of just how smart you really are. As you exhale, let go of the feeling of being stupid. Keep breathing in and out until you know for sure the feeling that you know is wrong for you is no longer part of your body. Once the new feeling or thought is locked into your body, you will feel happier and more positive about yourself and the world around you.

Remember, no matter what other people do or say to you or about you, you do not have to allow them to make you sad and unhappy.

You are in charge of creating a happy, loving world for yourself and others. You do this by first loving yourself and accepting the fact that you are perfect in every way. God made you perfect in every way.

Your affirmation for each day is: *"I am perfect in every way. God made me perfect in every way."*

6 • CLAIMING OUR PERSONAL POWER: UNCONDITIONAL LOVE

WHAT IS POWER?

What is power? Write down your feelings.

There are two kinds of power. First, there are those people who believe in power from outside sources. Can you think of any? (Money, social position, or a high position in government, religion, business)

How do you think these people would feel if their money or position were taken away?

The second type of power is our internal or spiritual power. This is the power that we get from knowing we are one with God and the universe. This is the power that we transmit as unconditional love and compassion for others.

With our personal power we can manifest many wonderful things for ourselves. We can use this power to manifest good health, happiness, loving friends and relationships or a nice home and other things for our comfort.

We can manifest for ourselves strength and security, confidence, courage and feelings of self-worth. We can eliminate feeling afraid or worrying about things that have not yet happened.

WAYS WE GIVE AWAY OR TAKE OTHERS' POWER

Sometimes we give away our personal power. Have you heard that term before — giving away your power? Here are some examples.

• You have a friend at school who wants you to help her cheat on her homework. You don't want to do it, because you know it is wrong to cheat. Your friend says she will not be your friend ever again if you don't help her.

• If you help her, you are doing something that you know is wrong. It is going against your spiritual awareness. If you help her, you are giving your power away to her. If you do not, you may lose a friend but you keep your personal power and will most likely have a new, more wonderful and honest friend come into your life in return.

• Have you ever had a problem something like this where a friend wanted you to do something you knew was wrong but you did it anyway to help the friend? Were you afraid you would not have any friends, that you would be alone in the world? How did it make you feel when you did something you felt was wrong? When you let someone else talk you into something you really didn't want to do?

• Have you ever tried to make one of your friends do something they did not want to do? If so, then you were trying to take their power from them.

Remember: Listen to your feelings and act on what is right for you at the present time.

• Your friend is constantly teasing and poking fun at you. You like this friend, but you don't like the teasing. It is driving you crazy. You can deal with this in several ways:

•• You can get mad and tell the friend to stop or you won't be his/her friend anymore.

•• You can tease him/her back and probably make him/her angry.

•• You can lovingly ask him/her to stop, explaining how it makes you feel.

Now put yourself in each of these pictures. What would you do?

You give your power away when you let others get the best of you or control you. If you lovingly settle your problems, you keep your power and your friends at the same time.

Remember: Know when to pay attention to your own needs and when to be selfless. Understand the effect your actions have on others and then choose what actions to take.

• Your friend is very unhappy whenever you are playing with other people. He/she thinks you should play only with him/her. How would you deal with this friend?

Remember: You are not responsible for other people's happiness. Each of us creates our own happiness by our choices. We are responsible only for ourselves.

• You want to get the support of your classmates in winning the position of class president. How would you go about getting that support?

• What you give out, you get back. If you give support to your classmates — helping them win different class titles, get on the soccer team, cheer them on in the spelling bee and so on, that support will come back to you tenfold.

Remember: Give to others what you want to receive – love, support, appreciation, healing, acknowledgment – and you will get more of the same in return.

• Another way we give our power away is by being afraid. Is there something you have felt afraid of lately that you would share with your mom or dad or friend? Or you can write down on a piece of paper what you are afraid of. What *is* fear? Fear is a feeling of heaviness, worry or concern. When you feel fear, learn to take courage and face it. God will always help you release and heal it. When you feel fear, sit quietly, relax your whole body and breathe deeply. Ask the universe, God, for guidance. "What can I do to change my fear?" God will always send help if you ask for it. This help may come through your thoughts, dreams, a book that you read, something you hear, a person. Help may come in many different ways, so keep your eyes and ears open.

Remember: To get rid of fear, turn and look right at it, and what you face will dissolve into light. Ask God to protect and help you.

• Your personal power comes from loving yourself for who you are right now, not who you will be at some time in the future. Many of us get into trouble when we try to be someone else or try to live up to the expectations that someone else sets for us. Here again we give up our power.

The best way to know yourself, to know your own personal power, is to sit quietly alone, away from other people who may influence you. Let your mind quiet down, then go inside and be one with your own energy, your higher-self energy. Let's take a moment and go inside

EXPERIENCING YOUR POWER

Sit quietly in a place where you will not be disturbed for a short time. Begin to breathe very deeply. As you breathe, put your attention in your toes, down in the very tips of your toes. How does the energy feel there?

Now bring your attention up into your feet, your ankles and heels. What does the energy feel like in these areas of your body?

Bring your attention up into the calves of your legs, your knees, thighs, hips. What does the energy feel like in these parts of your body? Does it feel the same or different from the energy in your feet and toes?

Now concentrate on the energy in your abdomen, stomach, chest, shoulders, upper arms, elbows, forearms, wrists, hands, fingers and thumbs. How does the energy feel in these parts of our body? Does the energy move faster as you move upward in your body? That's because the higher, more spiritual chakras are in the upper part of your body, and they spin at a much faster rate than your lower chakras.

Now focus your mind on your neck, face and head. How does the energy feel in these areas of your body?

You have experienced your own energy. Now take your attention above your head. Imagine that you are moving higher and higher, connecting with your higher self, a magical little golden ball of light just a few inches above your head. Hold your attention on this little golden ball for as long as you can. Think very loving thoughts. How does your energy feel now?

Remember: Love and accept who you are . . . not who you will be or who you think you should be.

LEARNING UNCONDITIONAL LOVE

Unconditional love means learning to be the source of love rather than waiting for others to be the source of love. It means keeping your heart open all the time. It means to let go of needing other people to give you things, to act in certain ways or respond with love. Some of us wait for other people to be loving before we will be loving ourselves in return.

Why do we need to learn to love unconditionally, loving someone without any conditions?

Unconditional love changes our fears. It takes courage to face things we are afraid of. It is often easier to see what our friends are afraid of than what we are afraid of ourselves. We don't like to admit to ourselves or others that we are afraid.

It is easier to see things in other people than in ourselves, so the universe often teaches us something about ourselves by putting other people in our life who show us what we need to learn.

WHERE DO OUR FEARS COME FROM?

Our fears come from our own thoughts. We may wonder:

• Did I disappoint someone?
• Do I feel I haven't tried hard enough?
• Do I feel I am not good enough?
• Do I feel I don't have enough friends?
• Do I feel I will not be successful in school?

What are some of your fears?

List them on a piece of paper so you become aware of what they are.

HERE ARE MY FEARS:

_____

_____

_____

_____

Fear is often covered up by thinking of reasons why something can't be done or believing that people are keeping us from doing something. We can blame it on other people; we can refuse to take responsibility; we can decide we can't do it anyway, so why try; we can get angry and quit — all because we are trying to cover up our fears.

If you are afraid of failing a test, for example, write down the reasons why you are afraid.

• I don't like the subject or teacher.
• I don't study enough.
• I forgot what to study, left my book at school and so on.

Then make an affirmation (a positive statement to repeat over and over): "I get an A on my math test." As you affirm this thought, this fear will dissolve into love and light.

If you move away from certain people for fear of their not wanting to be your friend, send love first to yourself to eliminate the fear, then send out unconditional love to those people. In other words, close your eyes and send yourself a ray of pink light and unconditional love. Then turn the ray from your heart and send it out to the people you are afraid of.

When you have the quality of unconditional love, you can smile when people do things that upset you and send them a warm, loving thought. Your sending them love keeps you from being affected by their behavior. Whatever you give out to others is a gift to yourself.

It is a big challenge to accept other people for who they are. If someone is sending angry or upsetting words to you, what can you do? That's right — send them warm, loving thoughts.

As you send love, you will raise your own energy vibration above that of the other person. Soon he/she will stop sending you energy you do not want, and you will find this situation not happening to you any more.

Forgiveness is also a part of unconditional love. Forgive yourself for the times during the day when you feel sad or angry or that you are not doing a good enough job. It is okay to feel that way. It is an emotion that we need to pay attention to. Then we need to forgive others for being angry or sad.

HOW CAN WE USE OUR POWER OF LOVE?

We can use our power of unconditional love in several ways. We can send love to people who are in pain or afraid. We can send love to people who make life miserable for those around them because these are the people most in need of love. We can send love to those who seem to have everything and to those who seem to have power over us. By using unconditional love, we can eliminate negative energy. Unconditional love is the most powerful emotion in this universe.

We use unconditional love to heal ourselves and others. We are like a magnet. When we give love, love comes right back to us.

Whenever you are afraid, imagine you are being held and loved by the most loving person you have ever known, a person who cares for you unconditionally, who loves you whether you feel good or bad, a person who is at your side all the time.

This person can be your higher self, your guardian angel, Jesus, God. You will always receive help from these beings of light whenever you call upon them.

Remember, these beings of light are always there for all of us no matter how we feel about ourselves or others. They are always there to help us even if we feel we haven't been good enough or not worthy of their love.

They are *always* ready to help us at any time, day or night. Call on your guardian angel, on Jesus, on God, on your higher self. Ask for help. You will see. They will be right there for you anytime you need them.

7 • CONNECTING WITH GOD AND CHANNELING HEALING ENERGY

CONNECTING WITH THE SOURCE

WHO IS THE SOURCE?

The Source — God — is the spirit energy that is in each and every one of us, in every part of our world and in every part of the entire universe. The Source is that energy we call God.

When you think of God, how do you see Him/Her? How do you feel about God?

We see and feel God as very powerful energy. But God is also very loving and kind. We see and feel Him/Her as loving, caring, helping. God is all-knowing, which means He/She knows everything about everyone and everything in the entire universe. And God is everywhere — in the largest planet to the tiniest grain of sand, God is there. God is in your house, in your friend's house, in your classroom — everywhere.

God represents good, kind and loving things. God represents the light we want to live in — the light of doing good, kind, loving, helpful things, of thinking and feeling good, kind, loving and helpful thoughts, of caring about other people and treating them like we would like to be treated.

When we live in the light or in a loving, positive way, we are happy, joyful and at peace with ourselves and the world in which we live. Everything seems to go our way. Because we are happy, sharing and caring ourselves, we bring happy, sharing and caring people into our lives.

God wants us to be just like Him/Her — happy, loving, caring, helpful, all-knowing, all-seeing, spreading joy and happiness and love everywhere we go.

We are working toward knowing all about ourselves and the world we live in, all about God and what God represents. We are one with God. And we can better know and feel this connection, this oneness, when we go inside ourselves in meditation.

WHERE IS THE SOURCE?

When you think about God, do you often wonder just exactly where God lives?

God is all around you. God is in the plants, the animals, the grass, the trees and the flowers. And God is within you.

If you get real quiet and listen very carefully, you can hear the soft, gentle voice of God offering you love and guidance. Listen . . . can you hear God's voice? Can you feel God's love around you?

CONNECTING WITH GOD

Let's go into the Source, or the part of God that lives within you, the same Source or God that is within each and every one of us. Let's be one with the light, the love, the power and the intelligence of God.

Relax your whole body as you breathe very deeply. Focus all your attention deep within yourself at your center. Let your mind and body be very quiet. Be as still and quiet as you can. Keep your eyes closed and concentrate very hard on your center — nothing outside of yourself, just your center.

Imagine a beautiful light in your center — a yellow, purple, blue or white light, whatever color you like the best. Imagine the light getting very, very large and very, very bright. Concentrate on the feeling of this light growing and becoming brighter within you. As the light gets larger and larger, how do you feel in your body? Are you feeling more and more energy? Do you feel very calm and peaceful?

Do you feel more loving and kind toward yourself and others?

Take a moment and see the light fill your center, and then see it fill your whole body with light, love and peace — the light, love and peace of God.

Now concentrate all your energy at your mind's eye, that spot in the center of your forehead between your eyebrows. Stare right at the back of your eyes, at your third eye. Picture a beautiful blue light getting brighter and much, much larger. Let the light expand until you begin to see a picture. This is a picture of God. God will appear in different ways to different people, or He/She may not appear at all. Let the picture come in as clearly as you can.

What colors do you see?

What shapes do you see? How do you see God?

Listen very carefully to God as He/She speaks to you. If you want to ask a question or receive help with a problem, ask God very quietly for assistance. Then listen very, very carefully, as quietly as you can. A small, quiet, loving voice will speak to you. Wait patiently for the answer. If you do not hear, feel or know the voice, do not be upset or think you did something wrong. Keep practicing. Do this meditation over and over and soon you will hear God speak to you.

Now let your eyes open very slowly and come back into the awareness of the room around you. Do you feel at peace? Do you feel now very happy, loving and kind?

Draw a picture of God as you saw Him/Her and label your picture the Source or God and then put the date on it. If you did not see God, use your imagination and draw a picture of God just as you think He/She looks.

Draw a picture of what you see in this meditation each time you do it. Be sure to write the date on your paper so you can compare your experiences as you practice.

Here's What God Looks Like to Me: (Draw a picture of God from your meditation experience. Put a date on this paper.)

CHANNELING LOVE & LIGHT

When we speak of *channeling*, we are talking about bringing energy in from other places, such as the spiritual plane, where your spirit guides and teachers live. Because we are always connected to the Source, or God, as you learned in a previous chapter, we can draw down, or channel, God's energy to heal ourselves and others.

LOVE AND LIGHT

Join hands with a friend or a group of friends. Imagine the top of your head opening up like a little window to receive the love and light of God. Bring the light down (channel the light) through your body. You will begin to feel more and more loving energy in your body.

Focus your attention on your heart center. Imagine that you are passing some light and love from your heart to the person on your right. When that person feels the love and light from you, he/she will pass the energy on to the next person in the circle until each person sitting in the circle has received the love and light energy.

As each of you receive the love and light from one another, each of you will feel lighter and more loving. In fact, the entire room will be filled with light and love.

Now think of someone you know who needs some extra-special love and light. Send that person some of your love and light to make them feel better.

The love and light of God is always available to each and every one of us and each and everything on the planet and in the universe. All we have to do is concentrate on bringing that love and light down into us and it is there.

Try channeling love and light to someone who is mean to you or who makes you feel badly. Or channel the love and light to someone you know who is unhappy or sad. You can help them feel better and much happier.

Channel the love and light to yourself when you are feeling afraid, angry or sad, then feel yourself become happier.

CHANNELING HEALING ENERGY

We are one with God. We come from God when we are born. When we die or pass over, we return to God for rest. Because we are one with God, it is easy for each and every one of us to channel, or bring down, the healing energy from God to help heal ourselves, our friends, parents, brothers and sisters, other people and even plants and animals.

You can feel this healing energy. Rub the palms of your hands together until they are very warm. Now separate your hands, palms facing each other, and pull them apart very, very slowly until they are about five to six inches apart. Do you feel a tingling, magnetic energy between the palms of your hands — an energy that seems to pull your hands toward each other or to fill a space between your hands?

If you have a plant at home that is feeling kind of puny or sickly, place your hands on the plant and channel this energy into it. You will notice the plant getting better and better.

You can do this healing energy work with friends who are not feeling well, with family members and even your pets. Simply rub the palms of your hands together and then place them on the person's or animal's body part that is feeling the distress — head, leg, stomach and so on.

Before you know it, the person, plant or animal will look and feel better. You do great work!

8 • BEYOND THE PHYSICAL BODY

TRAVELING OUT OF BODY

There is much more to ourselves than the body we can see as we read this. You learned about the aura in Chapter 3. The aura is the field of energy outside our physical bodies. It is made up of our emotions (happy, angry, sad, loving, playful, energetic, tired and so on). It is also made up of our thoughts and feelings, and it helps connect us to God through our spiritual body, the outermost part of our aura.

As you will remember, the aura is made up of colors that we can see when we look just outside the physical body. The colors you see are from each of our chakras, or energy centers.

We are very comfortable with our physical bodies. We know the physical body is there because we can see it, feel it, hear it, taste and smell it.

We can also feel, see, hear, smell and taste with our energy body, but it is more difficult to understand how it does these things, since we cannot sense it so easily with our physical selves. If you rub your hands together and then move your hand very slowly over your body or the body of a friend (about six to eight inches away from the physical body), you will be able to feel the outside edge of the aura.

We can travel in our energy body much more easily than in our physical body. Have you ever felt as though you were flying over the city or out into space? Have you ever seen yourself sitting across from your body and looking over at your body or looked down on your body from the ceiling, wondering, what is going on here?

You were actually traveling in your energy body, experiencing what is called an *out-of-body experience*. We can travel great distances in our energy body, which is connected to our physical body by a long silver cord. Our energy body always comes back to our physical body, unless it is time for our physical body to die. Then our energy body travels to the light of the Source and becomes one with the world of spirit, where our friends and relatives go after their physical bodies die. Our energy body lives on and on.

At night while we sleep it is a natural thing for our energy body (or spirit body) to leave our physical body to rest itself while it communicates with other spirit friends and teachers. It is a process as natural as our heartbeat or our breath. There may be times while we are playing that we will see our physical body from across the room or wherever we happen to be.

We can also use our minds to will our energy body to leave our physical body and then travel to different parts of the city, the state, the country, the world. We can even travel out across the universe, up to God, passing other planets and star systems on our way.

• Have you ever found yourself up on the ceiling or in a corner of the ceiling of your room?

- Have you ever looked down and seen yourself sleeping in your bed?
- In your awareness, have you ever traveled in your energy body to another part of the world or out into space?
- What types of experiences have you had in leaving your physical body?
- Have you seen yourself floating above your physical body?
- Have you seen yourself sitting on the other side of the room while your physical body is sitting or sleeping?
- Have you ever imagined yourself flying over the countryside?

TRAVELING MEDITATION

You can now do a special meditation, imagining your physical body disappearing into light. Then you can take a short journey with your mind and in your energy body to your favorite place.

First, think about where you would like to go. Think about your favorite place. Make a clear picture of this place in your mind. It could be Disneyland, the park, the zoo, Marine World, another country . . . anyplace you want to visit.

Before you begin, imagine that you are surrounded in God's love and light, that God is all around you, keeping you safe and protected. Now begin breathing deep, relaxed breaths as you close your eyes. Be very, very still.

Feel your toes and feel them disappear into light. Feel your feet and feel your feet disappear into light.

Feel your legs. Feel them disappear into light. You can no longer feel your physical feet, toes and legs. Now feel your body disappear into light from your hips on up through your abdomen, your stomach, your chest. Then feel your shoulders disappear into light.

Now let your arms and hands disappear into light. Finally, visualize your neck and head disappearing into light. Your whole body has now disappeared into light.

If you will notice, there is only your energy body left, wrapped in God's light. You can see, hear, feel, taste and smell in your energy body even better than you can in your physical body.

Imagine your energy body moving up and out the top of the head of your physical body. Move from side to side. Move up and down in your energy body.

Feel how easily you can move about. Feel how light you are. Look down at your hands and arms and legs and feet. How do you look in your energy body? Do you see the long silver cord that is attached to your physical body?

Let yourself rise up into a corner of the ceiling. Look down and all around the room you are in. When you are ready, rise even higher. Rise through the ceiling and the roof, on up into the sky above.

Your Energy Body

Think about the place you want to visit. Suddenly you are there. See this place. Feel this place. Hear all the sounds of this place. Taste and smell this place. You are actually at the place you have chosen to visit! Isn't that great? Doesn't it feel wonderful to be so free? You can travel anywhere you want as quickly as you want, because in energy form, there is no such thing as time and space. Think about where you want to be, and you are there.

Now bring yourself back to your house and let yourself drift gently back down through the roof and into the room where your physical body lies. Drift down and allow your energy body to enter at the top of the head of your physical body and back down into your physical body, moving around until you are comfortably back in your regular place.

When you are comfortable and back in your physical body, allow yourself to feel it and slowly begin to move around. Open your eyes.

- Could you feel yourself disappear into light?
- Could you feel your energy body leave your physical body and then look down and see your physical body below you?
- Did you see your spirit or energy body?
- What did it look like to you?
- Did you visit your favorite place?

Draw a picture of your favorite place just as you saw it in your energy body. Draw a picture of you in your energy body.

WHAT IS REINCARNATION?

Now that you are aware of your energy (spirit) body, you will better understand the concept of *reincarnation*.

Reincarnation simply means that after you die you come back and live another life in a different physical body, but with the same energy body that left the physical body when it died before.

For example, if you had lived in the time of Abraham Lincoln and the Civil War as a boy and you died during this time in history, you might be here again, but this time as a girl.

You might also return as a boy again, but you would look different. You would be dressed differently, have different colored hair and eyes and physical features. You could have a different skin color and live in a different part of the world.

You would have different parents, relatives and friends, but the parents, relatives and friends are most probably the same people you knew or were related to in some way in another lifetime.

This is sometimes very difficult to understand. It is a bit confusing, I admit. I will explain the idea of reincarnation to you more clearly as we go on.

After your physical body dies, you live in the spirit world with God, your friends and relatives who have died before you, and your spirit guides and guardian angels. You rest and play there in that beautiful, peaceful world in your energy body. Your physical body stays on Earth and is usually buried in the Earth or taken care of by other customs of your people.

Just before it is time for you to take another physical body, you sit down with your friends and relatives and guides in the spirit world and decide on the next lesson you want to come to Earth to learn. You decide how you intend to learn this lesson. That is, you decide what types of things you will experience at home, at work and at play, what types of people you will deal with, what kind of relationships you will encounter. Everything is designed to help you learn the particular lesson you choose that will help you move closer to God.

You choose the spirit guides you want to bring with you who will help you learn your lesson. There may be a very special guardian angel who specializes in helping people learn a certain type of lesson, and this angel is dedicated to helping you stay safe as you learn.

There may be a certain spirit guide who helps you with your spiritual growth and learning, one who helps you be more creative and use your imagination better. There may be a guide who can help you in your chosen field of work — doctor, nurse, electrician, scientist, teacher, writer and such.

You choose whoever you want to be your mom and your dad, your brothers and sisters, your relatives and friends, with their agreement, of course.

You choose those people who will influence your learning your chosen lesson.

Your mother in this lifetime could have been your aunt, your sister or even your daughter, son, father or brother in another lifetime.

Your father could have been your brother, sister, mother, uncle, son or daughter in another lifetime.

Many times we share a new life with those most familiar to us in a previous lifetime. It is as though in the beginning when we first came to Earth to learn lessons, we formed a spiritual family. We remain connected to that spiritual family until we complete all our Earthly lessons and return to God.

As you come to Earth you begin your lessons in life. Some lessons seem to be very difficult and other lessons easy. Your life can become more simple or more easy if you stay happy and positive in your thinking and deal with negative thoughts and feelings in a loving way.

Each lifetime offers you one more step up the ladder in your spiritual growth as you move closer to your one goal — becoming part of God's loving energy once again. You came from God and you will return to God when your lessons are completed. This is the goal of all souls.

SPIRIT GUIDES AND GUARDIAN ANGELS

Each of us has a special guardian angel or spirit guide/teacher who comes into this lifetime with us to help us as we grow and learn. They help us learn by directing us toward certain experiences, ideas, people and physical teachers. They guide us away from things that may be harmful to us and help us stay happy and loving.

You probably have already seen your guides. If not, you will soon be able to see and work more closely with him/her.

Guides appear in different forms. First, you must remember that they are not in a physical body. They might look like little balls of colored lights zooming around the room.

They might come in the form of an angel, glowing in pure white-and-gold light. You might seem to know them from somewhere else when they appear in the form of a person from a different land — Chinese, Indian, Roman, Greek, Russian, Scots and so on.

Sometimes they wear really different clothing and appear rather strange to us. But they are always very loving, kind and helpful. They are our best friends.

• Have you seen your guides or guardian angels?
• What do they look like?
• Have you heard their name(s)?

It is very easy to meet your spirit guides if you have not already encountered them.

GUIDES AND ANGELS

Lie on the floor, keeping your spine in a very straight line. Begin to breathe very slowly and calmly, focusing your attention on your center. Let your whole body begin to quiet down and relax.

Keep breathing very deep, relaxed breaths until your mind is still. If any thoughts come, simply let them pass right out the other side of your mind. Do not hold on to the thoughts.

Imagine yourself rising higher and higher, up to the clouds. Over to the right in the sky is a beautiful cloud with a magical garden. Float over to this cloud and enter this beautiful garden.

As you look around you will see many brightly colored flowers, a crystal pond with golden fish swimming around. There are a lot of crystals and brightly colored stones on the ground, and there is a feeling of total love and happiness, a feeling of being very close to God.

To your right is a crystal path. Begin walking down this path in your imagination. At a distance you will see a figure approaching you. This is one of your spirit guides or your guardian angel. As you get closer and closer, you will feel a very special kind of love. Send love to this guide or angel from your heart center in the form of a beam of pink light as well as very loving feelings.

- *Look at this guide or angel. What does he/she look like?*
- *Does it look like a person?*
- *Is it just colored lights?*
- *Does he/she wear special clothing or a robe?*
- *Does he/she have a hat on?*
- *What colors do you see around him/her?*
- *Is he/she very tall or very short?*
- *Ask for a name. If you are not given a name, it is okay.*

Now hold out your hand. Your guide/angel has a very special gift for you today. Look down at the gift. It may be a special crystal, a book, a symbol, a word or two. Thank your guide for the gift and give your him/her a big hug. They really like lots of love from us. Then turn and walk back down the path, back into the garden and over to the cloud that brought you to the garden.

Let your soft cloud drift back down to your room very, very gently. You will remember the guide you met today. You will remember his/her name if you were given a name, and you will remember the very special gift you were given, because you are special, too.

Now open your eyes and be back in the room at the present time.

DRAW A PICTURE OF WHAT YOUR SPIRIT GUIDE OR GUARDIAN ANGEL LOOKS LIKE FROM YOUR MEDITATION (put the date on your paper).

9 • WORKING WITH CRYSTALS AND STONES

LEARNING TO USE CRYSTALS AND STONES

Millions of years ago when Earth was formed, there appeared the first quartz crystal. It was made from gases deep within the Earth, mixed with very hot (over 200 degrees) seawater loaded with minerals.

According to legends, the ancient Lemurian and Atlantean peoples used crystals to channel the cosmic force into Earth through huge pyramid generators. They used this power to operate their cities, in healing work and in communication with their forefathers from another galaxy.

The Atlantean people realized how great the crystal power was and were developing this power for destructive purposes when the continent of Atlantis sank beneath the sea forever. Before this destruction, however, a few of the Atlantean people known as the "wise ones" programmed their great knowledge into crystals and sent the crystals to live deep within the Earth. These people knew that at just the right time in the future, certain people on Earth would find these special crystals and would be able to tune in to the secrets of this lost world. These crystals are the record keepers — crystals that you may even have in your own collection — crystals that have a small perfect triangle etched on one of the faces.

The few survivors of Atlantis traveled to Egypt, South America and Tibet, where they built pyramids just like those in Atlantis. You can still see the remains of these pyramids in these countries today.

Many ancient people throughout history have used colored stones and crystals to cure specific illnesses, for power and protection. Mayans and Native Americans used crystals to diagnose and treat disease and to see into their past and future lives. Certain native Mexicans believed that if you led a good life, after you died your soul went into a crystal and a person who found the crystal would enjoy good health and good luck throughout his/her lifetime, and that the crystal would serve as a guide.

Today crystals are used in wristwatches, computers, radio and television transmitters, lasers and many more technical devices. The crystal is popular because it has both negative and positive charges, and it can vibrate to any electrical current in a very precise manner.

Those of us working on our spiritual selves at this time have found that crystals can help us in meditation, in protection and guidance. We can put them under our pillow at night for a deeper understanding of our dreams. And we can use them to balance our body's energy system. They can change our feelings from sad to glad, give us more energy, help us focus and concentrate, and help us connect more closely to God. Crystals are light. They help bring more light into our lives.

PARTS OF A CRYSTAL

A quartz crystal has six sides on what is called the *body* of the crystal. These sides meet at the top in a sharp point called the *termination*.

In a single-terminated crystal, there is only one point, or termination. The base is flat or ragged-looking. This type of crystal grows out of rock, and only one point can be formed as it grows. In this type of crystal, energy enters the crystal at the base and moves up and out of the top, or termination.

In a double-terminated crystal, there are two points, or terminations. These types of crystals grow in soft, sandy soil, so the points can grow at both ends. In this type of crystal the energy flows in and out at both ends. It is used to balance our chakra centers.

WHAT CAN CRYSTALS DO?

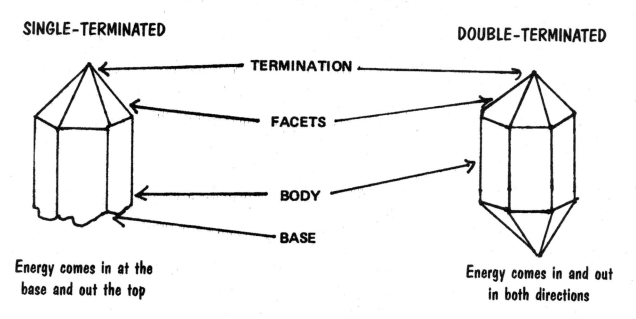

SINGLE-TERMINATED

DOUBLE-TERMINATED

TERMINATION

FACETS

BODY

BASE

Energy comes in at the base and out the top

Energy comes in and out in both directions

Crystals can *amplify our thoughts and feelings*. For instance, you can sit right now and think a happy thought. Be as happy as you can. Remember this feeling.

Now hold a crystal in your hand and again think a happy thought. Be as happy as you can. Do you feel even more happy now with the crystal helping you?

Crystals can *transform* the molecular structure of anything they are placed in contact with. Thus when we are holding or wearing a crystal, it can help by giving us more energy, balance and by healing our bodies as it removes negative thoughts from our energy field.

Crystals can *store* energy for us to use at a later time. When you charge crystals in the sunlight, for example, you are putting more energy into the stones. This energy will remain in the crystals until you are ready to use that energy in meditation, healing, protection and so on.

Crystals help us *focus.* If you hold a crystal during meditation, you can go deeper into your relaxed, meditative state.

We can use crystals to *transfer* energy to another person. We can do mental telepathy with crystals.

EXERCISE

Choose a partner. Sit on the floor facing each other about one or two feet apart. Choose one person to be the sender and the other the receiver. The sender should hold a crystal with the flat base against the third eye, pointing the tip of the crystal toward the receiver. The receiver should hold the point of the crystal to his/her third eye and the flat base pointing toward the sender.

Choose a color. The sender should send the color he/she chooses through the crystal to the receiver. The receiver should try to keep his/her mind clear and wait for the color to come in through his/her crystal. Try using numbers, letters, shapes and so on.

Then the receiver should play the role of sender and the sender the receiver. Be sure to change the position of your crystals depending on whether you are sender or receiver.

Remember . . . not everyone can receive or send equally well. Some of us are better senders. Some of us are better receivers. Find out what is easiest for you. Be happy with the great job you do in either position.

SELECTING A CRYSTAL

The best way to select a crystal or stone for yourself is to go to a crystal store and pick up the first one that seems to call to you, no matter how pretty or ugly it seems to be.

Hold the crystal in your left hand. Feel the energy. Does the energy make you feel good? Does it make you tingle all over? Do you feel like dancing? This is the crystal you should buy.

If you don't feel the energy with your left hand, try using your right hand. Left-handed people should test crystal energy with their right hand. Right-handed people should test crystal energy with their left hand.

When you pick up a crystal, remember that perhaps many different people have held that same crystal. Blow three times into the crystal before you check out its energy. Then only your own energies will be on the crystal. That way you will have an even better feeling about whether or not you want to buy this crystal.

WAYS TO USE YOUR CRYSTALS AND STONES

TUNING IN TO YOUR CRYSTALS AND STONES

Hold your crystal or stone in your left hand (right hand if you are left-handed). Feel the energy in your body. Where does the energy go? Where does the energy stop? Does your body feel hot or cold? Do you feel lots of energy? Is it peaceful? Sad? Happy?

Place the crystal or stone on your third eye. What do you see? What do you feel? What do you hear?

Now place that crystal or stone on any part of your body where it feels comfortable. Why did you place it there? How did it make you feel when you put it there?

You can do this exercise with each stone or crystal that you buy so you have a better understanding of how you are to use the stones for yourself and other people.

CLEANSING AND CHARGING YOUR CRYSTALS AND STONES

When you first buy a crystal or stone, remember that it has the energy of everyone who has touched it. In order not to pick up other people's energy and to work better with the stone, you must first cleanse the other people's energies out of the crystal or stone, and then it will be ready for you to work with and place your own energies within it.

There are many ways in which you can cleanse and charge your crystals/stones:
- Place the crystals and stones in sea salt for two to seven days.
- Rinse the crystals and stones in cold running water and place them in the sunlight or light of the full moon for three hours. The sunlight brings strong masculine energy and the moonlight brings soft, nurturing feminine energy.
- Hold the crystal/stone to your third eye and send the thought into the stone that it is clear, that there is no one else's energy in it.
- Hold the crystal/stone in front of you and blow hard into the stone, send the thought that it is clear of all other energy.

When you charge the crystal or stone with sunlight or moonlight, you refresh its power to focus, enhance and direct energy when you work with it. Its energies are refreshed, kind of like when you get up from a nice, long nap.

PROGRAMMING YOUR CRYSTAL

To program your crystal means that you place inside the crystal/stone the thought about how you want to use it. For example, if you want to heal yourself with the stone or crystal, program it by saying, "You are now programmed with healing energy for me, _____ (your name) . . ." This makes the crystal/stone a stronger tool for healing yourself.

You can program your crystal for meditation, to help you stay happy, to help you release negative or fearful thoughts and feelings, to help bring you good luck, better grades at school, healing energy for yourself and others, protection and so on.

To program your crystal, hold it to your third eye and have a mental image of what you want to put into the crystal. You can also hold the crystal to your heart center and send the loving thoughts into the crystal about what you want to work on with the crystal or stone.

You can blow three times with your breath into the crystal, at the same time thinking what you want to place inside it. Keep thinking the thought until you feel the message is locked tightly into the crystal or stone.

The programmed thought will stay in your crystal until you cleanse it by using one of the techniques we listed above. Then it will be ready for another program or thought of your choice.

CRYSTALS AS JEWELRY

You can wear crystals around your neck for protection against negative thoughts and feelings. While you wear or even carry a crystal, it is helping keep all your body's energies aligned and balanced so you feel more energized.

You can also wear any colored stone you wish. There may be one day you choose to wear a red stone and another day to wear green, depending on how you are feeling on any particular day. Let your own intuition tell you what color to wear and see how much better you feel as the day goes by.

CRYSTALS IN HEALING

If you have a pain in a certain part of your body, you can place a crystal or stone on the area to take away the pain. You can also do this for someone else. If you use a crystal, place the base on the part of your body that hurts and point the tip outward to send the excess energy of that part of your body, which appears as pain, out through the tip of the crystal.

Your intuition will tell you which of your colored stones to place on your body when there is a problem or when you are not feeling well. Place all of them on the table and let your hand be drawn to the one(s) you need.

CRYSTALS IN MEDITATION

Hold a crystal in your hand while you meditate. The crystal will help you relax more and quiet your mind.

Try lighting a candle and holding the crystal in front of the flame. Keep your eyes open and stare inside the crystal at the lights and colors until your eyes want to close naturally. See how long you can hold the colors in the center of your forehead behind your eyes — in your third-eye vision.

GOING INSIDE YOUR CRYSTAL

As you close your eyes, imagine that you can float right through an open doorway and into your crystal. You are now inside your crystal. It is like a little crystal house.

Look all around the inside of your crystal. Look at all the colors inside. What do you see?

Now feel your crystal. Feel the floor and the walls. How does the crystal feel?

Listen very carefully. What do you hear inside your crystal? Do you hear any sounds at all? Music?

What does it smell like inside your crystal?

What does it taste like inside your crystal? You may even want to place your tongue on one of the walls to find out.

Now sit quietly inside your crystal and just be one with it. Feel the peace all around you. Feel the energy of the crystal as it makes you feel more energized and happier, more at peace, more one with God.

When you are ready, let your body float back out of the doorway of the crystal, back into your room and into your physical body. Then open your eyes very slowly.

What did you think about your journey? What did you see? What did you feel? What did you hear? What did you smell? What did you taste? Draw a picture of your experience during the crystal meditation and put the date on your paper.

BALANCING YOUR CHAKRAS WITH CRYSTALS AND STONES

We discussed the chakras in a previous section of this workbook and the importance of keeping them in balance in order to maintain a healthy mind and body.

One way to keep your chakras balanced is by using crystals and stones that are the same color as the chakra on which you are placing the stones. For example, on your third eye (which is indigo or purple), you would place a dark blue or purple stone. On your solar plexus (which is yellow), you would place a yellow stone.

The more common stones you can use are as follows:
- 1st (root) chakra — red jasper or black onyx
- 2nd (hara) chakra — orange carnelian
- 3rd (solar plexus) chakra — yellow citrine
- 4th (heart) chakra — rose quartz or green aventurine
- 5th (throat) chakra — turquoise, aquamarine, blue-lace agate
- 6th (third eye) chakra — amethyst or sodalite
- 7th (crown) chakra — clear quartz crystal

You can place the stones on your body by yourself, or have a partner help you. It is important to lie down in a quiet place to do this so you can relax and feel the energy of the stones as they work on your body's energy systems.

To begin with, place the clear quartz with the point or termination touching the top of your head. Then place a stone on your third eye, one on your throat, on your heart, solar plexus, second chakra, and finally your root chakra. Leave the stones on for about fifteen minutes. Should one or more of the stones fall off your body, leave them off. The stones know better than we do when they have completed the task at hand.

You can place the stones on your body whenever you feel a bit out of touch with the world — nervous, hyperactive, angry, sad, when you don't feel really good all over, when you feel stuck places or blockages in your body, when you can't concentrate and so on. Your intuition will let you know when it is time for a chakra balance.

When you have completed the balance, you may want to place your stones in cold running water and sunlight to cleanse, recharge and refresh their energies. Take good care of your stones and they will take great care of you. They are just like loving little friends.

CHAKRA BALANCING WITH STONES

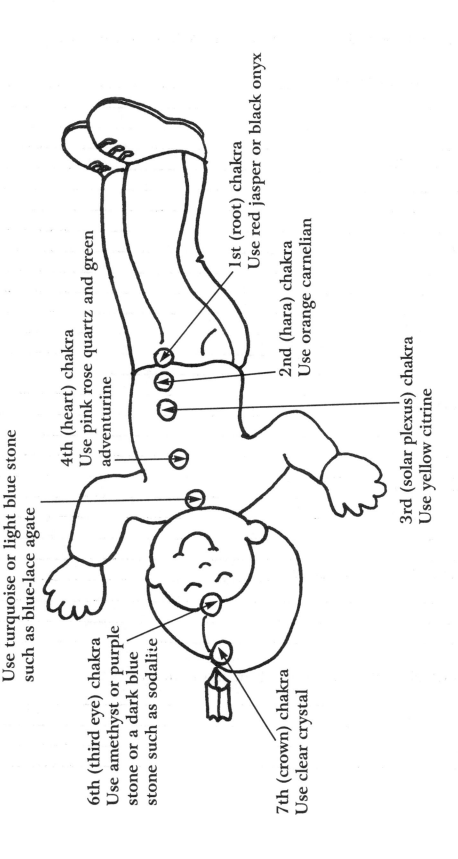

5th (throat) chakra
Use turquoise or light blue stone
such as blue-lace agate

4th (heart) chakra
Use pink rose quartz and green
adventurine

6th (third eye) chakra
Use amethyst or purple
stone or a dark blue
stone such as sodalite

7th (crown) chakra
Use clear crystal

1st (root) chakra
Use red jasper or black onyx

2nd (hara) chakra
Use orange carnelian

3rd (solar plexus) chakra
Use yellow citrine

What did you feel in your chakra centers during the balancing?

First (root) chakra _____
_____
_____

Second chakra _____
_____
_____

Third chakra _____
_____
_____

Fourth chakra _____
_____
_____

Fifth chakra _____
_____
_____

Sixth chakra _____
_____
_____

Seventh (crown) chakra _____
_____
_____

In which chakra did you feel the most energy?

_____
_____
_____
_____

10 • THE WORLD OF DREAMS

WHAT IS A DREAM?

Every night, whether you are aware of it or not, you dream. Some dreams are in color and some are in black and white. Still other dreams may have only one or two colors, such as purple and green, red and orange, or any single color or combinations of colors.

Dreaming is important to us. Dreams help us understand more about ourselves, perhaps what has gone on in a previous life or lives. Dreams give us messages about what is happening in our current life. Dreams even help us to understand better a certain situation or problem and offer solutions. Dreams can help us with events that will take place in the future. Dreams are messages about you and what is going on with you.

TYPES OF DREAMS

Some dreams are called *physical dreams.* This kind of dreams tells you about what is going on in your body — whether you need to change your diet, visit a doctor, get more rest, read a certain book and so on.

For example, if you see yourself in the kitchen eating candy, ice cream and all kinds of junk food and you are very fat and not feeling good, the dream could be telling you to change your diet, that all this stuff you have been eating is not good for you. The dream is helping you understand that if you keep eating so much junk food, you will not feel well, could get sick and might become very fat.

There are dreams called *literal dreams.* These dreams are like a movie video. They play back for you the events that took place the day before you dreamed. The dream makes you pay attention to certain things that have occurred so you can understand them better.

For example, you dream that one of your very best friends is treating you very mean and you are unhappy about it. You don't understand why the friend is mean. When you awaken and think about the dream, you realize you were mean to your friend at school yesterday. The dream is showing you what took place and putting you in your friend's place at school so you can feel how that friend felt. This is a lesson so you don't treat people badly. When *you* know how it feels, you are less apt to do something to others that would make *you* feel bad. You don't like the feeling, and neither do the people you are mean to.

You can also experience a *spiritual dream.* This dream takes place when you talk to angels, Jesus or the Source, see spirit guides and talk to them while dreaming. These kinds of dreams show you that you are doing well in your spiritual growth. They can also show you that when you are patient, understanding, kind, loving and forgiving, great things come to you, bringing you more happiness, joy and good feelings.

Sometimes our dreams take us back into a lifetime that we lived before. These dreams are called *reincarnation dreams.* They often present to us people from a foreign country who speak a different language than ours. If you dream like this, often you are seeing into one of your past lives, a life that has an important influence or message for your present life. You should pay special attention to the action that takes place so you can see how similar that lifetime was to this one.

Sometimes you have the same dream more than once. This is called a *repeating dream.* When this happens it means you have not understood the message that came in the first dream. Pretty soon the message is made clear enough so you understand the dream's message and then the dream will not return. It can also happen to make sure that you will remember it. These dreams often come in threes.

If you have a dream that tells you about something that is going to happen the next day, the next week or even some time in the future, you are experiencing what is called a *precognitive dream.* This kind of dream makes you aware of a coming event so you can be ready to experience it.

A *lucid dream* is one where you seem to be perfectly aware that you are asleep and are controlling or consciously changing what happens during it.

There may be times when you experience a *nightmare.* Nightmares involve events that happen during the day prior to the dream. For instance, you might have a nightmare from watching a scary television program.

If something disturbing or frightening is going on in your life, you may dream about ghosts, monsters or ugly creatures. The creatures, ghosts and monsters represent your fears. Nightmares are perfectly normal. They put us in touch with our greatest fears so we can change them.

If you dream about death, it does not necessarily mean that someone is gong to die. Death represents changes, a change from some old idea or belief to something new. We all need to make changes for our growth, and sometimes those changes are represented in dreams as a death . . . the death of the *old* way of thinking and believing.

If you dream of falling or running, it often means that you are falling down on your job or running away from a responsibility. If you dream about running away from a friend, is there a favor a friend asked you to do that you agreed to, but then did something else instead? It shows that you are running away from your responsibility to your friend.

Dreams are very important to us, so it is very important for us to understand them. To understand your dreams, first you must remember them, and that is not always easy to do.

First, some dreams are just not very interesting, so we simply forget about them.

Second, the dreams may make us too uncomfortable, so we let go of that dream as well.

Third, we sometimes wake up very fast, perhaps because we are late for school. We dash out of bed and don't give our minds time to concentrate on our dreams.

Fourth, might dismiss the dream as unimportant.

Fifth, we might have a difficult time understanding the *symbols* that come in our dreams.

Our subconscious mind, the part of our mind that is hidden, the part we don't think about, speaks to us in symbols, which are the pictures you see in your dreams. A symbol is something that stands for something else.

For example, an eagle might suggest power or freedom. An owl might stand for wisdom, "the wise old owl." The White House could represent a thought about the President or the United States government or leadership.

When you dream about a house or a building, you are usually dreaming about yourself. The basement represents your subconscious mind. The main floor represents your conscious mind, the mind you are aware of as you think during the day. The upstairs or attic represents your higher self, or that part of you connected to the Source, God.

A car dream is interesting, because the car usually represents your physical body. If you dream about your car running out of gas, it could mean that your body is running out of energy and you need more rest, that you are tired.

Also, this type of dream could be a precognitive dream. It could mean that you should check your family car because you might not have enough gas to get where you are going. Check the gas gauge on your car, and also check your own feelings about your body to see which type of dream you had.

WORKING WITH DREAMS

There are some very simple rules to make it easier to remember, understand and interpret your dreams so you can start working with your dreams right away.

• **You yourself are every person and every object in your dream.** When you dream of someone other than yourself, your dream is usually not about that person, but about what that person may mean to you and/or the qualities or traits that the two of you have in common.

For example, you both may be honest and dependable, good students and so on. Dreaming about this friend is pointing out those qualities in yourself.

When you dream about a man, your dream is showing you the qualities in yourself that are masculine, such as being a good leader, taking control, being strong.

If your dream is about a woman, the dream is showing you the qualities in yourself that are loving, caring nurturing and soft.

- **Think of the dream first as something that exists physically, and then think of the dream as symbols.**

For instance, if you dream about your car running out of gas, first check your car to make sure it has plenty of gas. Then, since the car represents your physical self, make sure you are not too tired, that you are not running out of gas.

- **Always look at your dream as a lesson to improve on yourself, to make yourself an even better person than you already are.**

- **Tell your dream to someone else.** It helps to get another person's idea and opinion. In telling it out loud you may notice or remember something that you had forgotten.

- **Act upon your dreams.** If your dream is showing you how you need to improve on yourself, follow the suggestions. If your dream is suggesting that you need more rest, then go to bed early until you feel less tired.

- **Finish your dreams or have someone help you finish them.** Whenever you wake up crying or yelling for help from a scary dream, immediately make up a pleasant ending or have your mom or dad help you make one up. Then go back to sleep and finish your dream in a pleasant way — with a happy ending.

- **Tell yourself to repeat any dream you don't understand.** If you have a dream that you don't understand, even with help from others, when you go to sleep the next night, tell yourself out loud, "I would like this dream to come again with the same message, but in a way that will be easier for me to understand." You can do this every night until you understand its message.

- **Keep a record of your dreams and go over them on occasion.** Keep a notebook by your bed so you can write down what you dream. This helps you remember them and understand how your unconscious mind uses particular symbols by the patterns you will eventually see.

THINGS TO THINK ABOUT IN UNDERSTANDING YOUR DREAMS

There are a few things you need to think about when you get ready to interpret your dreams:

- What is the setting? Is the dream taking place at home, at school, in a vacation spot? Is it warm and sunny or cool, rainy, stormy?
- Who are the people in your dream? Mom and Dad? Your brothers and sisters? Your friends, your teacher? Your relatives? Or people you don't know?
- What action is taking place in your dream? What are you or the others doing? Watching TV, working, playing, running, flying, swimming?
- What colors appear in your dream? Are there mostly bright colors, or dark, muddy-looking colors? Do the colors change?
- How do you feel about the dream? Does it make you happy, sad, peaceful? Do you feel angry?
- What was said by the people in the dream? Try to remember the words.
- What other thoughts and feelings do you have about this particular dream? Is there anything you don't understand? Is there one particular part of the dream that you really have strong feelings about?

Practice working on your dreams for a couple of weeks and see how good you get in a very short time. Your dreams are magic mirrors of what is going on in your life, and in that subconscious mind we call our secret self. Dreams help us understand those secrets.

It is also beneficial to have a dreamwork dictionary for interpreting the symbols. You can usually find many good books at local metaphysical and other bookstores.

In the dream dictionary, you can look up the main symbol in your dream and see if the meaning in the dictionary gives you a more clear understanding of your own dream. Always look up the main symbol — those symbols that really jump out at you and stick in your mind. These are the keys for unlocking the mystery about what your subconscious mind is trying to tell you through your dreams.

The following page is a dream worksheet you can copy and use to record your dreams.

MY DREAM WORKSHEET

1. What is the main word, words, person, symbol, action, and so on, that I remember most from my dream?

   _____

   _____

2. What is the scenery around where my dream takes place? (House, school, beach, forest, hospital, restaurant, auto shop, and so on.)

   _____

   _____

3. Who are the people I see in my dream? (friends, family, relatives, myself). Are they men or women, boys or girls?

   _____

   _____

4. What did the people say in the dream?

   _____

   _____

5. What is going on in my dream? What is the action taking place? (Running, flying, sleeping, playing with friends or animals, traveling, learning at school, going to a restaurant or grocery store and so on.)

   _____

   _____

6. What are the colors I see in my dream? Do they change or stay the same color?

   _____

   _____

7. How do I feel when I think about my dream? (Happy, sad, peaceful, calm, spiritual, a little excited or afraid?)

   _____

   _____

8. What are my thoughts about what this dream means to me?

_____

_____

9. Is this a physical dream about me and my body's condition?

_____

_____

10. Is this dream reminding me of something I need to learn from my experience from the day before?

_____

_____

11. Is this dream about my spiritual growth and how I am learning?

_____

_____

12. Do I feel it is a precognitive dream — that it is about something that is going to really happen in a day, week, month, and so on?

_____

_____

13. Is this a nightmare? Was I afraid of something before I went to sleep?

_____

_____

14. Is this a dream that I have had before — a repeating dream? Do I need to pay special attention to this dream?

_____

_____

15. Did I feel I saw myself in a past life? What was the message?

_____

_____

16. Was I out of body and traveling, actually visiting the places I thought I was only dreaming about?

_____

_____

AFTERWORD

This is by no way the end, but rather the beginning of a wondrous journey into light. Each meditation and exercise offered in this workbook is intended for you to practice, practice, practice. And as you do so, a wondrous new world will continue to avail itself to you and your family.

By now you have become aware of a world little known and little understood by most — the world of non-physical energy. This energy is God's energy, energy which each and every one of us has available for our own personal use in helping ourselves heal and grow and in helping others. This wonderful energy is made up of God's wisdom, knowledge and unconditional love, which each of us has the power to tune into when we get quiet and ask for him/her to speak to us.

Planet Earth is now in the midst of a great change. The vibration of unconditional love is beginning to alter Earth's former pattern of separateness. And you are all a part of this great transformation. As you grow, as you change and bring more light into your being, more love into your heart for yourself and all mankind, you can help transform Earth into a more loving and beautiful place. Let your heart light shine out into the world, into the hearts of others, into the universe. And as your love flows forth into the lives of others, your life will truly become loving and joyful as well.

In love and light,

Leia

ABOUT THE AUTHOR

The '80s were a decade of self-discovery for Leia Stinnett after she began researching many different avenues of spirituality. In her profession as a graphic designer she had become restless, knowing there was something important she had to do outside the materiality of corporate America.

In August 1986 Leia had her first contact with Archangel Michael when he appeared in a physical form of glowing blue light. A voice said, "I am Michael. Together we will save the children."

In 1988 she was inspired by Michael to teach spiritual classes in Sacramento, California, the Circle of Angels. Through these classes she had the opportunity to work with learning-disabled children, children of abuse and those from dysfunctional homes.

Later Michael told her, "Together we are going to write the Little Angel Books." To date Leia and Michael have created thirteen Little Angel Books that present various topics of spiritual truths and principles. The books proved popular among adults as well as children.

The Circle of Angels classes have been introduced to several countries around the world and across the U.S., and Leia and her husband Douglas now have a teacher's manual and training program for people who wish to offer spiritual classes to children. Leia and Michael have been interviewed on Canadian Satellite TV and have appeared on NBC-TV's *Angels II — Beyond the Light,* which featured their Circle of Angels class and discussed their books and Michael's visit.

The angels have given Leia and Douglas a vision of a new educational system without competition or grades — one that supports love and positive self-esteem, honoring all children as the independent lights they are. Thus they are now writing a curriculum for the new "schools of light" and developing additional books and programs for children.

BOOK MARKET

A reader's guide to the extraordinary books we publish, print and market for your enLightenment.

NEW!
THE EXPLORER RACE

Robert Shapiro/Zoosh

In this expansive overview, Zoosh explains, "You are the Explorer Race. Learn about your journey before coming to this Earth, your evolution here and what lies ahead." Topics range from ETs and UFOs to relationships.

$25.00 Softcover 574p   ISBN 0-929385-38-1

NEW!
ETs AND THE EXPLORER RACE

Robert Shapiro/Joopah

The next book in the famous Explorer Race series. Covers the Grays, abductions, the genetic experiment, UFO encounters, contactees, the future of our relationship with various ETs and much more.

$14.95 softcover   ISBN 0-929385-79-9

BEHOLD A PALE HORSE

William Cooper

Former U.S. Naval Intelligence Briefing Team Member reveals information kept secret by our government since the 1940s. UFOs, the J.F.K. assassination, the Secret Government, the war on drugs and more by the world's leading expert on UFOs.

$25.00 Softcover 500p   ISBN 0-929385-22-5

◆ BOOKS BY LIGHT TECHNOLOGY RESEARCH

SHINING THE LIGHT

Revelations about the Secret Government and their connections with ETs. Information about renegade ETs mining the Moon, ancient Pleiadian warships, underground alien bases and many more startling facts.

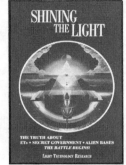

$12.95 Softcover 208p   ISBN 0-929385-66-7

SHINING THE LIGHT
BOOK II

Continuing the story of the Secret Government and alien involvement. Also information about the Photon Belt, cosmic holograms photographed in the sky, a new vortex forming near Sedona, and nefarious mining on sacred Hopi land.

$14.95 Softcover 422p   ISBN 0-929385-70-5

SHINING THE LIGHT
BOOK III

The focus shifts from the dastardly deeds of the Secret Government to humanity's role in creation. The Earth receives unprecedented aid from Creator and cosmic councils, who recently lifted us beyond the third dimension to avert a great catastrophe.

$14.95 Softcover 512p   ISBN 0-929385-71-3

🌐 LIGHT TECHNOLOGY'S BOOKS OF LIGHT

THE SEDONA VORTEX GUIDEBOOK

by 12 channels

200-plus pages of channeled, never-before-published information on the vortex energies of Sedona and the techniques to enable you to use the vortexes as multidimensional portals to time, space and other realities.

$14.95 Softcover 236p   ISBN 0-929385-25-X

NEW!
THE ALIEN PRESENCE

Evidence of secret government contact with alien life forms.

Ananda

Documented testimony of the cover-up from a U.S. president's meeting to the tactics of suppression. The most complete information yet available.

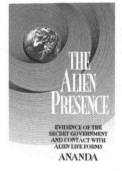

$19.95 Softcover   ISBN 0-929385-64-0

COLOR MEDICINE

The Secrets of Color Vibrational Healing

Charles Klotsche

A practitioner's manual for restoring blocked energy to the body systems with specific color wavelengths by the founder of "The 49th Vibrational Technique."

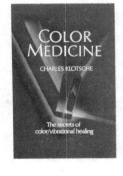

$11.95 Softcover 114p   ISBN 0-929385-27-6

◆ BOOKS BY DOROTHY ROEDER

THE NEXT DIMENSION IS LOVE

Ranoash

As speaker for a civilization whose species is more advanced, the entity describes the help they offer humanity by clearing the DNA. An exciting vision of our possibilities and future.

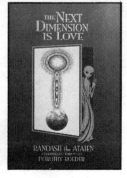

$11.95 Softcover 148p   ISBN 0-929385-50-0

REACH FOR US

Your Cosmic Teachers and Friends

Messages from Teachers, Ascended Masters and the Space Command explain the role they play in bringing the Divine Plan to the Earth now!

$14.95 Softcover 204p   ISBN 0-929385-69-1

CRYSTAL CO-CREATORS

A fascinating exploration of 100 forms of crystals, describing specific uses and their purpose, from the spiritual to the cellular, as agents of change. It clarifies the role of crystals in our awakening.

$14.95 Softcover 288p   ISBN 0-929385-40-3

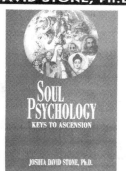

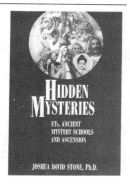

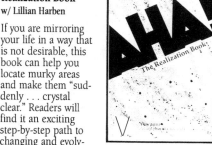
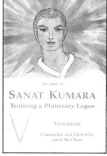

BOOK MARKET

A reader's guide to the extraordinary books we publish, print and market for your enLightenment.

✦ BOOKS BY LYNN BUESS

CHILDREN OF LIGHT, CHILDREN OF DENIAL

In his fourth book Lynn calls upon his decades of practice as counselor and psychotherapist to explore the relationship between karma and the new insights from ACOA/ Co-dependency writings.

$8.95 Softcover 150p   ISBN 0-929385-15-2

NUMEROLOGY FOR THE NEW AGE

An established standard, explicating for contemporary readers the ancient art and science of symbol, cycle, and vibration. Provides insights into the patterns of our personal lives. Includes life and personality numbers.

$11.00 Softcover 262p   ISBN 0-929385-31-4

NUMEROLOGY: NUANCES IN RELATIONSHIPS

Provides valuable assistance in the quest to better understand compatibilities and conflicts with a significant other. A handy guide for calculating your/his/her personality numbers.

$12.65 Softcover 239p   ISBN 0-929385-23-3

THE STORY OF THE PEOPLE
Eileen Rota

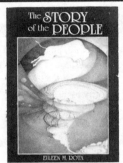

An exciting history of our coming to Earth, our traditions, our choices and the coming changes, it can be viewed as a metaphysical adventure, science fiction or the epic of all of us brave enough to know the truth. Beautifully written and illustrated.

$11.95 Softcover 209p   ISBN 0-929385-51-9

THE NEW AGE PRIMER
Spiritual Tools for Awakening

A guidebook to the changing reality, it is an overview of the concepts and techniques of mastery by authorities in their fields. Explores reincarnation, belief systems and transformative tools from astrology to crystals.

$11.95 Softcover 206p   ISBN 0-929385-48-9

LIVING RAINBOWS
Gabriel H. Bain

A fascinating "how-to" manual to make experiencing human, astral, animal and plant auras an everyday event. Series of techniques, exercises and illustrations guide the reader to see and hear aural energy. Spiral-bound workbook.

$14.95 Softcover 134p   ISBN 0-929385--42-X

LIGHT TECHNOLOGY'S BOOKS OF LIGHT

ACUPRESSURE FOR THE SOUL
Nancy Fallon, Ph.D.

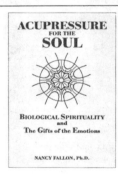

A revolutionary vision of emotions as sources of power, rocket fuel for fulfilling our purpose. A formula for awakening transformation with 12 beautiful illustrations.

$11.95 Softcover 150p   ISBN 0-929385-49-7

✦ BOOKS BY RUTH RYDEN

THE GOLDEN PATH

"Book of Lessons" by the master teachers explaining the process of channeling. Akashic Records, karma, opening the third eye, the ego and the meaning of Bible stories. It is a master class for opening your personal pathway.

$11.95 Softcover 200p   ISBN 0-929385-43-8

LIVING THE GOLDEN PATH
Practical Soul-utions to Today's Problems

Guidance that can be used in the real world to solve dilemmas, to strengthen inner resolves and see the Light at the end of the road. Covers the difficult issues of addictions, rape, abortion, suicide and personal loss.

$11.95 Softcover 186p   ISBN 0-929385-65-9

✦ BOOKS BY WES BATEMAN

KNOWLEDGE FROM THE STARS

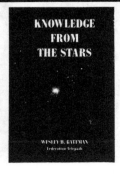

A telepath with contact to ETs, Bateman has provided a wide spectrum of scientific information. A fascinating compilation of articles surveying the Federation, ETs, evolution and the trading houses, all part of the true history of the galaxy.

$11.95 Softcover 171p   ISBN 0-929385-39-X

DRAGONS AND CHARIOTS

An explanation of spacecraft, propulsion systems, gravity, the Dragon, manipulated Light and interstellar and intergalactic motherships by a renowned telepath who details specific technological information received from ETs.

$9.95 Softcover 65p   ISBN 0-929385-45-4

FOREVER YOUNG
Gladys Iris Clark

You can create a longer younger life! Viewing a lifetime of a full century, a remarkable woman shares her secrets for longevity and rejuvenation. A manual for all ages. Explores tools for optimizing vitality, nutrition, skin care via Tibetan exercises, crystals, sex.

$9.95 Softcover 109p   ISBN 0-929385-53-5

BOOK MARKET

A reader's guide to the extraordinary books we publish, print and market for your enLightenment.

ORDER NOW!
1-800-450-0985
or Fax 1-800-393-7017
Or use order form at end

◆ BOOK AND MEDITATION TAPES by VYWAMUS/BARBARA BURNS

CHANNELLING:
Evolutionary Exercises for Channels

A lucid, step-by-step guide for experienced or aspiring channels. Opens the self to Source with simple yet effective exercises. Barbara has worked with Vywamus since 1987.

$9.95 Softcover 118p

ISBN 0-929385-35-7

THE QUANTUM MECHANICAL YOU

Workshop presented by the *Sedona Journal of Emergence!* in Sedona April 2-3, 1994

Barbara Burns through Vywamus explores the "mutational" process that humanity agreed to undertake at the time of the Harmonic Convergence. This fundamental biochemical and electromagnetic restructuring is necessary for those who have agreed to remain in body throughout the full shift. The "mutation" process is a complete reformatting of the human DNA.

B101-4 (6-tape set) $40

◆ BOOKS BY SCOTT FREE

Transformational channeled poetry for the New Age removes past blockages — opens up memories of all that you are. Must reading for all lightworkers.

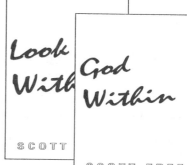

LOOK WITHIN
If you are committed to changing your life, let your soul guide you to look within. Powerful!
$9.95 Softcover 108p   ISBN 0-9635673-0-6

GOD WITHIN
Dedicated to those who want powerful transformation and to be their God within. Illuminating!
$11.95 Softcover 120p

◆ BOOK AND MEDITATION TAPES by BRIAN GRATTAN

MAHATMA I & II
Brian Grattan

Combined version of the original two books. Guidance to reach an evolutionary level of integration for conscious ascension. Fascinating diagrams, meditations, conversations.

$19.95 Softcover 328p

ISBN 0-929385-77-2

DNA FOR THE MULTIDIMENSIONAL MATRIX

Brian Grattan's
Mahatma
Seminar

Seattle Seminar, October 27-30, 1994

These 12 powerful hours of meditations lead to total spiritual transformation by recoding your 2-strand DNA to function in positive mutation, which finite scientists refer to as "junk" DNA. Ancient intergalactic civilizations altered humanity's DNA; the ultimate achievement now for Earth's inhabitants is to spiritualize the 12-strand DNA to achieve complete universal and monadic consciousness; these audio tapes are a profound step in that direction.

M102-12 $79.95 (12-tape set)

LIGHT TECHNOLOGY'S BOOKS OF LIGHT

◆ MEDITATION TAPES AND BOOKS by YHWH/ARTHUR FANNING

ON BECOMING
YHWH through Arthur Fanning

Knowing the power of the light that you are. Expansion of the pituitary gland and strengthening the physical structure. Becoming more of you.
F101 $10

HEALING MEDITATIONS/ KNOWING SELF
Knowing self is knowing God. Knowing the pyramid of the soul is knowing the body. Meditation on the working of the soul and the use of the gold light within the body.
F102 $10

MANIFESTATION & ALIGNMENT with the POLES
Alignment of the meridians with the planet's grid system. Connect the root chakra with the center of the planet.
F103 $10

THE ART OF SHUTTING UP
Gaining the power and the wisdom of the quiet being that resides within the sight of thy Father.
F104 $10

CONTINUITY OF CONSCIOUSNESS
Trains you in the powerful state of waking meditation.
F105 $25 (3-tape set)

NEW! SOULS, EVOLUTION AND THE FATHER
Channeling Lord God Jehovah

Lucifer's declaration begins the process of beings thinking another is greater than self. About the creation of souls; a way to get beyond doubt; how souls began to create physical bodies.

Finally in stock!

$12.95 Softcover 200p   ISBN 0-929385-33-0

SIMON

A compilation of some of the experiences Arthur has had with the dolphins, which triggered his opening and awakening as a channel.

$9.95 Softcover 56p   ISBN 0-929385-32-2

THE SOUL REMEMBERS
A Parable on Spiritual Transformation
Carlos Warter, M.D.

What is the purpose of human life? What is the reality of this world I find myself in?
A cosmic perspective on essence, individuality and relationships. Through the voices of archetypes of consciousness, this journey through dimensions will assist the reader to become personally responsible for cocreating heaven on Earth.

$14.95 210p   ISBN 0-929385-36-5

MEDICAL ASTROLOGY
Eileen Nauman, DHM

The most comprehensive book ever on this rapidly growing science. Homeopath Eileen Nauman presents the Med-Scan Technique of relating astrology to health and nutrition. With case histories and guide to nutrition.

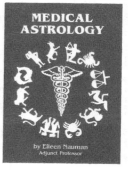

$29.95 339p   ISBN 0-9634662-4

BOOK MARKET

A reader's guide to the extraordinary books we publish, print and market for your enLightenment.

✦ BOOKS by HALLIE DEERING

LIGHT FROM THE ANGELS
Channeling the Angel Academy

Now those who cannot attend the Angel Academy in person can meet the Rose Angels who share their metaphysical wisdom and technology in this fascinating book.

$15.00 Softcover 230p   ISBN 0-929385-72-1

DO-IT-YOURSELF POWER TOOLS

Assemble your own glass disks that holographically amplify energy to heal trauma, open the heart & mind, destroy negative thought forms, tune the base chakra and other powerful work. Build 10 angelic instruments worth $700.

$25.00 Softcover 96p   ISBN 0-929385-63-2

PRISONERS OF EARTH
Psychic Possession and Its Release
Aloa Starr

The symptoms, causes and release techniques in a documented exploration by a practitioner. A fascinating study that demystifies possession.

$11.95 Softcover 179p   ISBN 0-929385-37-3

✦ RICHARD DANNELLEY

SEDONA POWER SPOT, VORTEX AND MEDICINE WHEEL GUIDE

Discover why this book is so popular! Six detailed maps, special meditations for each power spot, and a lot of heart. Richard Dannelley is a native of the Sedona area.

$11.00 Softcover 112p   ISBN 0-9629453-2-3

NEW! SEDONA: BEYOND THE VORTEX
The Ultimate Journey to Your Personal Place of Power

An advanced guide to ascension, using vortex power, sacred geometry, and the Merkaba.

$12.00 Softcover 152p   ISBN 0-9629453-7-4

THIS WORLD AND THE NEXT ONE
Aiello

A handbook about your life before birth and your life after death, it explains the how and why of experiences with space people and dimensions. Man in his many forms is a "puppet on the stage of creation."

$9.95 Softcover 213p   ISBN 0-929385-44-6

LIGHT TECHNOLOGY'S BOOKS OF LIGHT

✦ BOOKS by TOM DONGO

NEW! MERGING DIMENSIONS
with Linda Bradshaw

The authors' personal experiences. 132 photographs of strange events, otherworldly beings, strange flying craft, unexplained light anomalies. *They're leaving physical evidence!*

$14.95 Softcover 200p   ISBN 0-9622748-4-4

UNSEEN BEINGS UNSEEN WORLDS

Venture into unknown realms with a leading researcher. Discover new information on how to communicate with nonphysical beings, aliens, ghosts, wee people and the Gray zone. Photos of ET activity and interaction with humans.

$9.95 Softcover 122p   ISBN 0-9622748-3-6

THE LEGEND OF THE EAGLE CLAN
Cathleen M. Cramer with Derren A. Robb

This book brings a remembrance out of the past . . . magnetizing the lost, scattered members of the Eagle Clan back together and connecting them on an inner level with their true nature within the Brotherhood of Light.

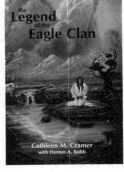

$12.95 Softcover 281p   ISBN 0-929385-68-3

THE ALIEN TIDE
The Mysteries of Sedona II

UFO/ET events and paranormal activity in the Sedona area and U.S. are investigated by a leading researcher who cautions against fear of the alien presence. For all who seek new insights. Photos/illustrations.

$7.95 Softcover 128p   ISBN 0-9622748-1-X

THE QUEST
The Mysteries of Sedona III

Fascinating in-depth interviews with 26 who have answered the call to Sedona and speak of their spiritual experiences. Explores the mystique of the area and effect the quests have had on individual lives. Photos/illustrations.

$8.95 Softcover 144p   ISBN 0-9622748-2-8

THE MYSTERIES OF SEDONA

An overview of the New Age Mecca that is Sedona, Arizona. Topics are the famous energy vortexes, UFOs, channeling, Lemuria, metaphysical and mystical experiences and area paranormal activity. Photos/illustrations.

$6.95 Softcover 84p   ISBN 0-9622748-0-1

BOOK MARKET

A reader's guide to the extraordinary books we publish, print and market for your enLightenment.

◆ BOOKS by ROYAL PRIEST RESEARCH

PRISM OF LYRA

Traces the inception of the human race back to Lyra, where the original expansion of the duality was begun, to be finally integrated on earth. Fascinating channeled information.

$11.95 Softcover 112p   ISBN 0-9631320-0-8

VISITORS FROM WITHIN

Explores the extra-terrestrial contact and abduction phenomenon in a unique and intriguing way. Narrative, pre-cisely focused chan-neling & firsthand accounts.

$12.95 Softcover 171p   ISBN 0-9631320-1-6

PREPARING FOR CONTACT

Contact requires a metamorphosis of consciousness, since it involves two species who meet on the next step of evolution. A channeled guidebook to ready us for that transformation. Engrossing.

$12.95 Softcover 188p   ISBN 0-9631320-2-4

SOUL RECOVERY & EXTRACTION
Ai Gvhdi Waya

Soul recovery is about regaining the pieces of one's spirit that have been trapped, lost or stolen either by another person or through a traumatic incident that has occurred in one's life.

$9.95 Softcover 74p   ISBN 0-9634662-3-2

I'M O.K. I'M JUST MUTATING!
The Golden Star Alliance

Major shifts are now taking place upon this planet. It is mutating into a Body of Light, as are all the beings who have chosen to be here at this time. A view of what is happening and the mutational symptoms you may be experiencing.

$6.00 Softcover 32p

OUR COSMIC ANCESTORS
Maurice Chatelain

A former NASA expert documents evidence left in codes inscribed on ancient monuments pointing to the exist-ence of an advanced prehistoric civilization regularly visited (and technologically assisted) by ETs.

$9.95 Softcover 216p   ISBN 0-929686-00-4

LIGHT TECHNOLOGY'S BOOKS OF LIGHT

◆ BOOKS by PRESTON NICHOLS with PETER MOON

THE MONTAUK PROJECT
Experiments in Time

The truth about time that reads like science fiction! Secret research with invisi-bility experiments that culminated at Montauk, tapping the powers of creation and manipulating time itself. Exposé by the technical director.

$15.95 Softcover 156p   •   ISBN 0-9631889-0-9

MONTAUK REVISITED
Adventures in Synchronicity

The sequel unmasks the occult forces that were behind the technology of Montauk and the incredible characters associated with it.

$19.95 Softcover 249p   ISBN 0-9631889-1-7

PYRAMIDS OF MONTAUK
Explorations in Consciousness

A journey through the mystery schools of Earth unlocking the secret of the Sphinx, thus awaken-ing the consciousness of humanity to its ancient history and origins.

$19.95 Softcover 249p   ISBN 0-9631889-2-5

ENCOUNTER IN THE PLEIADES:
An Inside Look at UFOs

For the first time, the personal history of Preston Nichols is revealed, also amazing information the world has not yet heard. An unprecedented insight into the tech-nology of flying saucers. Never has the complex subject of UFOs been explained in such simple language.

$19.95 Softcover   ISBN 0-9631889-3-3

ACCESS YOUR BRAIN'S JOY CENTER
Pete Sanders Jr.

An M.I.T.-trained sci-entist's discovery of how to self-trigger the brain's natural mood-elevation mechanisms as an alternative to alcohol, nicotine, drugs or overeating to cope with life's pres-sures and challenges. Combination book and audio cassette package.

$29.95 Softcover 90p plus tape   ISBN 0-9641911-0-5

PRINCIPLES TO REMEMBER AND APPLY
Maile

A handbook for the heart and mind, it will spark and expand your remem-brance. Explores space, time, relation-ships, health and includes beautiful meditations and affir-mations. Lucid and penetrating.

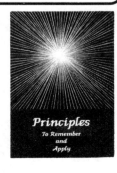

$11.95 Softcover 114p   ISBN 0-929385-59-4

BOOK MARKET

A reader's guide to the extraordinary books we publish, print and market for your enLightenment.

NEW!
A Dedication to the SOUL/SOLE GOOD OF HUMANITY
Maria Vosacek

To open awareness, the author shares information drawn from looking beyond the doorway into the Light. She explores dreams, UFOs, crystals, relationships and ascension.

DEDICATED TO THE SOUL/SOLE GOOD OF HUMANITY
MARIA VOSACEK

$9.95 Softcover 288p   ISBN 0-9640683-9-7

SEDONA STARSEED
Raymond Mardyks

There is a boundary between the dimensions humans experience as reality and the beyond. Voices from beyond the veil revealed a series of messages. The stars and constellations will guide you to the place inside where infinite possibilities exist.

SEDONA Starseed
A Galactic Unification
Raymond Mardyks

$14.95 Softcover 146p   ISBN 0-9644180-0-2

EARTH IN ASCENSION
Nancy Anne Clark, Ph.D.

About the past, present and future of planet Earth and the role humans will play in her progress. Nothing can stop Earth's incredible journey into the unknown. You who asked to participate in the birthing of Gaia into the fifth dimension were chosen!

EARTH IN ASCENSION

$14.95 Softcover 136p   ISBN 0-9648307-6-0

WE ARE ONE:
A Challenge to Traditional Christianity
Ellwood Norquist

Is there a more fulfilling way to deal with Christianity than by perceiving humankind as sinful, separate and in need of salvation? Humanity is divine, one with its Creator, and already saved.

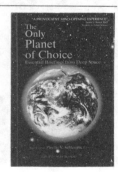
We Are One:
A Challenge to Traditional Christianity
By Ellwood Norquist

$14.95 Softcover 169p   ISBN 0-9646995-2-4

AWAKEN TO THE HEALER WITHIN
Rich Work & Ann Marie Groth

An empowerment of the soul, an awakening within and a releasing of bonds and emotions that have held us tethered to physical and emotional disharmonies. A tool to open the awareness of your healing ability.

Awaken To The Healer Within
by Rich Work with Ann Marie Groth

$14.95 Softcover 330p   ISBN 0-9648002-0-9

TEMPLE OF THE LIVING EARTH
Nicole Christine

An intimate true story that activates the realization that the Living Earth is our temple and that we are all priests and priestesses to the world. A call to the human spirit to celebrate life and awaken to its cocreative partnership with Earth.

Temple of the Living Earth
Nicole Christine
Crystal Priestess of Gaia

$16.00 Softcover 150p   ISBN 0-9647306-0-X

 # LIGHT TECHNOLOGY'S BOOKS OF LIGHT

THE ONLY PLANET OF CHOICE
Council of Nine through Phyllis V. Schlemmer

One of the most significant books of our time, updated. About free will and the power of Earth's inhabitants to create a harmonious world. Covers ET civilizations, the nature of the Source of the universe, humanity's ancient history etc.

The Only Planet of Choice
Essential Briefings from Deep Space
Phyllis V. Schlemmer

$14.95 Softcover 342p   ISBN 1-85860-023-5

INANNA RETURNS
V.S. Ferguson

A story of the gods and their interaction with humankind. Simple tale by Inanna, whose Pleiadian family, including Enlil and Enki, took over the Earth 500,000 years ago, this story brings the gods to life as real beings with problems and weaknesses, although technologically superior.

INANNA RETURNS
V.S. Ferguson

$14.00 Softcover 274p

IT'S TIME TO REMEMBER
Joy S. Gilbert

A riveting story of one woman's awakening to alien beings. Joy recounts her initial sightings, dreams and ongoing interaction with nonhuman beings she calls her friends. After her terror, she sees her experiences as transformative and joyful.

It's Time To Remember
A Riveting Story of One Woman's Awakening to Alien Beings
By Joy S. Gilbert

$19.95 Hardcover 186p*   ISBN 0-9645941-4-5

♦ MAGICAL SEDONA through the DIDGERIDOO by TAKA

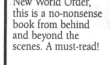
Magical Sedona through the Didgeridoo

Taka blends the sound of the Didgeridoo into the sacred landscape of Sedona, Arizona, describing different areas, joining with the characteristic animal and nature sounds he has experienced and recorded over the years. The drone of the Didgeridoo takes us into a state between conscious and unconscious; the joy of nature sounds and the human voice touches deeper levels in our beings and we are reconnected with all creation.

Each selection is approximately 10 minutes long and starts and ends at sunrise. The music will give you, wherever you are, the opportunity to tune in to the magic of Sedona.

1. *Cathedral Rock* • *Nurturing, beauty*
2. *Bell Rock* • *Energizing, guardian*
3. *Dry Beaver Creek* • *Inspiring, creative*
4. *Airport* • *Direction beyond limitation*
5. *Canyons* • *Sheltering, motherly*
6. *Sedona* • *Love*

T101 $12.00

LIFE ON THE CUTTING EDGE
Sal Rachelle

The most significant questions of our time require a cosmic view of reality. From the evolution of consciousness, dimensions and ETs to the New World Order, this is a no-nonsense book from behind and beyond the scenes. A must-read!

LIFE ON THE CUTTING EDGE
SAL RACHELE

$14.95 Softcover 336p   ISBN 0-9640535-0-0

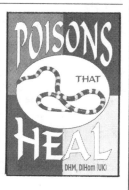

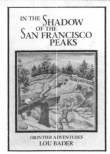

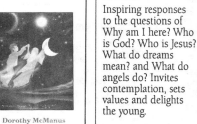

BOOKS PUBLISHED BY LIGHT TECHNOLOGY PUBLISHING

Title	Author	Price	No. Copies	Total
Acupressure for the Soul	Fallon	$11.95	_____	$ _____
Alien Presence	Ananda	$19.95	_____	$ _____
Arcturus Probe	Argüelles	$14.95	_____	$ _____
Behold a Pale Horse	Cooper	$25.00	_____	$ _____
Cactus Eddie	Gold	$11.95	_____	$ _____
Channelling	Vywamus/Burns	$ 9.95	_____	$ _____
Color Medicine	Klotsche	$11.95	_____	$ _____
ETs and the Explorer Race	Shapiro	$14.95	_____	$ _____
Explorer Race	Shapiro	$25.00	_____	$ _____
Forever Young	Clark	$ 9.95	_____	$ _____
Guardians of The Flame	George	$14.95	_____	$ _____
Great Kachina	Bader	$11.95	_____	$ _____
Legend of the Eagle Clan	Cramer	$12.95	_____	$ _____
Living Rainbows	Bain	$14.95	_____	$ _____
Mahatma I & II	Grattan	$19.95	_____	$ _____
Millennium Tablets	McIntosh	$14.95	_____	$ _____
New Age Primer		$11.95	_____	$ _____
Poisons That Heal	Nauman	$14.95	_____	$ _____
Prisoners of Earth	Starr	$11.95	_____	$ _____
Sedona Vortex Guide Book		$14.95	_____	$ _____
Shadow of San Francisco Peaks	Bader	$ 9.95	_____	$ _____
The Soul Remembers	Warter	$14.95	_____	$ _____
Story of the People	Rota	$11.95	_____	$ _____
This World and the Next One	Aiello	$ 9.95	_____	$ _____
LIGHT TECHNOLOGY RESEARCH/FANNING				
Shining the Light		$12.95	_____	$ _____
Shining the Light — Book II		$14.95	_____	$ _____
Shining the Light — Book III		$14.95	_____	$ _____
ARTHUR FANNING				
Souls, Evolution & the Father		$12.95	_____	$ _____
Simon		$ 9.95	_____	$ _____
WESLEY H. BATEMAN				
Dragons & Chariots		$ 9.95	_____	$ _____
Knowledge From the Stars		$11.95	_____	$ _____
LYNN BUESS				
Children of Light, Children of Denial		$ 8.95	_____	$ _____
Numerology: Nuances in Relationships		$12.65	_____	$ _____
Numerology for the New Age		$11.00	_____	$ _____

Title	Price	No. Copies	Total
RUTH RYDEN			
The Golden Path	$11.95	_____	$ _____
Living The Golden Path	$11.95	_____	$ _____
DOROTHY ROEDER			
Crystal Co-Creators	$14.95	_____	$ _____
Next Dimension is Love	$11.95	_____	$ _____
Reach For Us	$14.95	_____	$ _____
HALLIE DEERING			
Light From the Angels	$15.00	_____	$ _____
Do-It-Yourself Power Tools	$25.00	_____	$ _____
JOSHUA DAVID STONE, PH.D.			
Complete Ascension Manual	$14.95	_____	$ _____
Soul Psychology	$14.95	_____	$ _____
Beyond Ascension	$14.95	_____	$ _____
Hidden Mysteries	$14.95	_____	$ _____
Ascended Masters	$14.95	_____	$ _____
VYWAMUS/JANET McCLURE			
AHA! The Realization Book	$11.95	_____	$ _____
Light Techniques	$11.95	_____	$ _____
Sanat Kumara	$11.95	_____	$ _____
Scopes of Dimensions	$11.95	_____	$ _____
The Source Adventure	$11.95	_____	$ _____
Evolution: Our Loop of Experiencing	$14.95	_____	$ _____
LEIA STINNETT			
A Circle of Angels	$18.95	_____	$ _____
The Twelve Universal Laws	$18.95	_____	$ _____
Where Is God?	$ 4.95	_____	$ _____
Happy Feet	$ 4.95	_____	$ _____
When the Earth Was New	$ 4.95	_____	$ _____
The Angel Told Me To Tell You Goodby	$ 4.95	_____	$ _____
Color Me One	$ 4.95	_____	$ _____
One Red Rose	$ 4.95	_____	$ _____
Exploring the Chakras	$ 4.95	_____	$ _____
Crystals For Kids	$ 4.95	_____	$ _____
Who's Afraid of the Dark	$ 4.95	_____	$ _____
The Bridge Between Two Worlds	$ 4.95	_____	$ _____

BOOKS PRINTED OR MARKETED BY LIGHT TECHNOLOGY PUBLISHING

Title	Author	Price	No. Copies	Total
Access Your Brain's Joy Center (w/ tape)	Sanders	$29.95	_____	$ _____
Awaken to the Healer Within	Work, Groth	$14.95	_____	$ _____
A Dedication to the Soul/Sole. . .	Vosacek	$ 9.95	_____	$ _____
Earth in Ascension	Clark	$14.95	_____	$ _____
God Within	Free	$11.95	_____	$ _____
"I'm OK I'm Just Mutating"	Golden Star Alliance	$ 6.00	_____	$ _____
Innana Returns	Ferguson	$14.00	_____	$ _____
It's Time To Remember	Gilbert	$19.95	_____	$ _____
I Want To Know	Starr	$ 7.00	_____	$ _____
Life On the Cutting Edge	Rachelle	$14.95	_____	$ _____
Look Within	Free	$9.95	_____	$ _____
Medical Astrology	Nauman	$29.95	_____	$ _____
Our Cosmic Ancestors	Chatelain	$ 9.95	_____	$ _____
Out-Of-Body Exploration	Mulvin	$ 8.95	_____	$ _____
Peace Labyrinth	Bartnett	$ 9.95	_____	$ _____
Principles to Remember and Apply	Maile	$11.95	_____	$ _____
Sedona Starseed	Mardyks	$14.95	_____	$ _____
Song of Sirius	McManus	$ 8.00	_____	$ _____
Soul Recovery and Extraction	Waya	$ 9.95	_____	$ _____
Spirit of The Ninja	Siege	$ 7.95	_____	$ _____
Temple of The Living Earth	Christine	$16.00	_____	$ _____

Title	Author	Price	No. Copies	Total
The Only Planet of Choice	Schlemmer	$14.95	_____	$ _____
Touched By Love	McManus	$ 9.95	_____	$ _____
We Are One	Norquist	$14.95	_____	$ _____
Richard Dannelley				
Sedona Power Spot/Guide		$11.00	_____	$ _____
Sedona: Beyond The Vortex		$12.00	_____	$ _____
Tom Dongo: Mysteries of Sedona				
Mysteries of Sedona — Book I		$ 6.95	_____	$ _____
Alien Tide—Book II		$ 7.95	_____	$ _____
Quest—Book III		$ 8.95	_____	$ _____
Unseen Beings, Unseen Worlds		$ 9.95	_____	$ _____
Merging Dimensions		$14.95	_____	$ _____
Preston B. Nichols with Peter Moon				
Montauk Project		$15.95	_____	$ _____
Montauk Revisited		$19.95	_____	$ _____
Pyramids of Montauk		$19.95	_____	$ _____
Encounter in the Pleiades: Inside Look at UFOs		$19.95	_____	$ _____
Lyssa Royal and Keith Priest				
Preparing For Contact		$12.95	_____	$ _____
Prism of Lyra		$11.95	_____	$ _____
Visitors From Within		$12.95	_____	$ _____

ASCENSION MEDITATION TAPES

Title	No.	Price	No. Copies	Total
JOSHUA DAVID STONE, PH.D.				
Ascension Activation Meditation	S101	$12.00	_____	$ _____
Tree of Life Ascension Meditation	S102	$12.00	_____	$ _____
Mt. Shasta Ascension Activation Meditation	S103	$12.00	_____	$ _____
Kabbalistic Ascension Activation	S104	$12.00	_____	$ _____
Complete Ascension Manual Meditation	S105	$12.00	_____	$ _____
Set of all 5 tapes		$49.95	_____	$ _____
VYWAMUS/BARBARA BURNS				
The Quantum Mechanical You (6 tapes)	B101-6	$40.00	_____	$ _____
TAKA				
Magical Sedona through the Didgeridoo	T101	$12.00	_____	$ _____

Title	No.	Price	No. Copies	Total
BRIAN GRATTAN				
Seattle Seminar Resurrection 1994 (12 tapes)	M102	$79.95	_____	$ _____
YHWH/ARTHUR FANNING				
On Becoming	F101	$10.00	_____	$ _____
Healing Meditations/Knowing Self	F102	$10.00	_____	$ _____
Manifestation & Alignment w/ Poles	F103	$10.00	_____	$ _____
The Art of Shutting Up	F104	$10.00	_____	$ _____
Continuity of Consciousness	F105	$25.00	_____	$ _____
Black-Hole Meditation	F106	$10.00	_____	$ _____
Merging the Golden Light Replicas of You	F107	$10.00	_____	$ _____

BOOKSTORE DISCOUNTS HONORED — SHIPPING 15% OF RETAIL

❑ CHECK ❑ MONEY ORDER

CREDIT CARD: ❑ MC ❑ VISA

\# _____

Exp. date: _____

Signature: _____

(U.S. FUNDS ONLY) PAYABLE TO:

LIGHT TECHNOLOGY PUBLISHING

P.O. BOX 1526 • SEDONA • AZ 86339
(520) 282-6523 FAX: (520) 282-4130

1-800-450-0985
Fax 1-800-393-7017

NAME/COMPANY _____

ADDRESS _____

CITY/STATE/ZIP _____

PHONE _____ CONTACT _____

All prices in US$. Higher in Canada and Europe.

SUBTOTAL: $ _____

SALES TAX: $ _____
(7.5% – AZ residents only)

SHIPPING/HANDLING: $ _____
($4 Min.; 15% of orders over $30)

CANADA S/H: $ _____
(20% of order)

TOTAL AMOUNT ENCLOSED: $ _____

CANADA: DEMPSEY (604) 683-5541 Fax (604) 683-5521 • ENGLAND/EUROPE: WINDRUSH PRESS LTD. 0608 652012/652025 FAX 0608 652125
AUSTRALIA: GEMCRAFT BOOKS (03) 888-0111 FAX (03) 888-0044 • NEW ZEALAND: PEACEFUL LIVING PUB. (07) 571-8105 FAX (07) 571-8513

HOT OFF THE PRESSES AT . . .

LIGHT TECHNOLOGY PUBLISHING

— THE ASCENSION BOOK SERIES by Joshua David Stone —

THE COMPLETE ASCENSION MANUAL: How to Achieve Ascension in This Lifetime

BOOK I A synthesis of the past and guidance for ascension. This book is an extraordinary compendium of practical techniques and spiritual history. Compiled from research and channeled information, it offers specific steps to accelerate our process of ascension — here and now!

ISBN 0-929385-55-1 $14.95

SOUL PSYCHOLOGY: Keys To Ascension

BOOK II Modern psychology deals exclusively with personality, ignoring the dimensions of spirit and soul. This book provides ground-breaking theories and techniques for healing and self-realization.

ISBN 0-929385-56-X $14.95

BEYOND ASCENSION: How to Complete the Seven Levels of Initiation

BOOK III This book brings forth incredible new channeled material that completely demystifies the seven levels of initiation and how to attain them. It contains revolutionary new information on how to anchor and open our 36 chakras and how to build our light quotient at a rate of speed never dreamed possible.

ISBN 0-929385-73-X $14.95

HIDDEN MYSTERIES: An Overview of History's Secrets from Mystery Schools to ET

Contacts BOOK IV An exploration of the unknown and suppressed aspects of our planet's past, it reveals new information on the extraterrestrial movement and secret teachings of the ancient Master schools, Egyptians and Essenes.

ISBN 0-929385-57-8 $14.95

THE ASCENDED MASTERS LIGHT THE WAY: Keys to Spiritual Mastery from Those

Who Achieved It BOOK V The lives and teachings of forty of the world's greatest Saints and spiritual beacons provide a blueprint for total self-realization. Inspiring guidance from those who learned the secrets of mastery in their lifetimes.

ISBN 0-929385-58-6 $14.95

ASCENSION ACTIVATION TAPES:

How to anchor and open your 36 chakras and build your light quotient at a speed never dreamed possible. Hundreds of new ascension techniques and meditations directly from the galactic and universal core.

ASCENSION ACTIVATION MEDITATION TAPE	S101	$12.00
TREE OF LIFE ASCENSION MEDITATION TAPE	S102	$12.00
MT. SHASTA ASCENSION ACTIVATION MEDITATIONS	S103	$12.00
KABBALISTIC ASCENSION ACTIVATION	S104	$12.00
COMPLETE ASCENSION MANUAL MEDITATION	S105	$12.00
SET OF ALL 5 TAPES	S110	$49.95